GameWØrldz

For B + J + A

GameWØrldz

by Chuck Ian Gordon

Science Fiction Novel

English Translation
by Jan Wassermann-Fry

Version 1.7.52h_final_en

www.GameWØrldz.com, www.GameWØrldz.de,
www.GameWorldz.de

The German National Library (Deutsche Nationalbibliothek)
holds data about this book accessible via internet at:
http://dnb.dnb.de

Imprint

GameWØrldz
a science fiction novel
by Chuck Ian Gordon

www.GameWØrldz.com, www.GameWØrldz.de,
www.Gameworldz.de

Published and copyright © by:
Gordon's Arcade, Triftstr. 30, 61350 Bad Homburg, Germany
Website: www.GordonsArca.de

Text Copyright © 2010-2014 by Chuck Ian Gordon
Edited by: Ulrike Jonack
Proofreading and German typesetting by Heinz W. Pahlke
English Translation by Jan Wassermann-Fry
English Proofreading by Oliver Fry
All rights reserved.

First published 2012 in Germany. First English edition 2013

ISBN 978-3-944218-04-5 (eBook version)
ISBN 978-3-944218-05-2 (Print version)

Title cover, GameWØrldz logo and stock changes:
© Chuck Ian Gordon, © Tobias Roetsch – www.gtgraphics.de

used stock photos from www.fotolia.com:
© #11320134 and #11521138 Paul Moore, #27780276 diter,
#31341575 Jesse-lee-Lang, #36111736 katalinks
Font: Diavlo from Jos Buivenga   www.exljbris.com/diavlo.html

GameWØrldz™, 3futurez™ and Gordon's Arcade™
are trademarks of Gordon's Arcade

Table of Contents

Foreword to the English edition of GameWØrldz

Dear science fiction fan!

You hold in your hands the result of three years of several people's work and a considerable personal financial investment. Starting with a professional editor who herself loves and writes science-fiction, I was helped by a proofreader, a typesetter (for the print version), and an artist for the cover. And now GameWØrldz has been translated from German to English by a native speaker and proofread by another. And what for? Bragging? Well of course — or at least partially.

Yet there are some reasons that are much more important. The first reason is the idea, the story behind GameWØrldz. Besides the flying cars, which I included for fun, all the content of the story is highly realistic from my point of view. I just extrapolated my experience as an IT professional including my own experiments with artificial neural networks. Which means the questions the story poses are realistic as well and wait to be answered by all of us.

The second and most important reason is you. You, as science fiction enthusiast, are interested in our future. And you have the power to change the world for the better. I encourage you to do so. And this is why I've put so much effort into my work. Because you are worth it, because you can make a difference.

Finally I want you to have lots of fun reading this novel, which I intentionally designed to be like a Hollywood action movie in written form. I hope the motion picture comes alive in your head. If you like it, please spread the word. If you dislike it, please tell me what I could do to improve it. Either way I appreciate your feedback.

Now, enjoy reading and then go, change the world and build a better future for all of us.

Yours sincerely

Chuck Ian Gordon, December 8th 2013

P.S.: As my part of changing the future I am actively working on the sequel to GameWØrldz — called 3futurez. Besides the novel it will be produced as a real holodeck musical. Stay up-to-date by checking out: www.3futurez.com

Prologue: Quest

The night sky's moon and stars caused silver reflections on the desert river's gently rippling surface. The last glow of sunset faded on the horizon and then the darkness was complete. The day's heat slowly made way for a fresh wind blowing from the distant mountains. A palm-lined river snaked its way through the desert, past an Egyptian-style temple shaped like a pyramid with stone pillars on its porch. The temple's front was lit up by a path leading from the river to the entrance with twin rows of torches on either side of it, as well as the fires that burned in two enormous copper bowls.

None of the four men guarding the temple's entrance paid any heed to the tree trunk slowly floating downriver, nor to the five heads that were hiding behind it. The tree trunk slowly drifted towards the palm tree-covered riverbank near the temple in a soft arc. Under cover of darkness, five silhouettes rose from the water. The parched desert sand instantly absorbed any water droplets without a sound.

Taking the group's lead was the Herculean warrior, Haran. Dancing flames reflected faintly off his formidable helmet and armor of leather and steel. A few steps behind was Natasha, the bewitching battlemage, dressed in a stunning, rune-decorated robe that left little to the imagination with its mixture of low-cut dress and armor elements. She held a long wand in her right hand. Sneaking behind those two was Yicca, the cunning thief, with a short sword in each hand and plainer leather armor, but lined with knives and a selection of secret compartments, as well as multicolored ropes that were painted pitch-black by the darkness. Bringing up the rear were Martan and Zerbos, two warriors who knew each other from way before. They had joined the party of heroes at a tavern in a nearby village. Both wore chain mail and carried shield, ax and helmet. The heroes' mission was to find a magical artifact that was said to be stowed deep within the vaults beneath the temple.

Hidden from view by the palm trees, five shadows slipped along the right-hand wall of the temple, ready to subdue any guards. Having covered half the distance, a sudden noise from the river caused them to halt. A boat had just landed at the stone pier in front of the temple, and now an ominous-looking figure was hurrying towards the guards. A silver trident protruded from where the left hand should have been. The long cloak exuded an evil, black aura, highlighted only by the trident that glittered and a pale, bald head.

"Damnit!" whispered Haran. "Just what we needed. That's Gorth, the Dark Armies' second-in-command. According to legend, Gorth lost his hand in a fight against a mighty sea monster. His powers are not that strong, but his cunning is beyond belief. If he's personally guarding the temple, we can be sure it'll be well-defended."

Gorth walked up to one of the guards, who stood rigidly to attention, exchanged a few words, and then he vanished into the temple.

"Alright then," Haran whispered. "We'll do it as follows: Yicca, you climb to the top of the pyramid and surprise the guards from above. Meanwhile, Martan and Zerbos sneak around the temple and come at them from the left, while Natasha and I attack from the right. But you must wait for the signal — the usual birdcall."

Yicca nodded with a smile. They continued silently creeping through the palm grove until they had to part ways, Yicca proceeding to climb up the steep stone wall, Natasha and Haran briefly waiting out of sight behind the corner of the temple, and Zerbos and Martan sneaking on further around the back of the temple.

"Looks like it'll be more interesting than we first thought," whispered Natasha in Haran's ear with a smile.

This caused him to raise an eyebrow and ask himself: 'How could anyone draw enjoyment from such a dangerous mission?' This lack of concern often astounded him about Natasha. Sometimes he felt it was all just a game to her.

Yicca was already above the entrance; the other two were still behind the temple. A sudden scream cut through the nocturnal silence, and a pile of stones came crashing down next to the entrance, shortly followed by a frantically flailing Yicca. He hit the ground at the four guards' feet, causing a cloud of dust to rise from where he lay. Haran's mouth was agape in surprise. The guards drew their sabers and surrounded the motionless thief. Instinctively, Haran reacted, and stormed at the guards with an angry roar. With a metallic rasping sound he drew his massive two-handed greatsword and raised it high above his head in preparation for his first blow. The other temple guards watched in horror as the guard closest to Haran was cleaved in two in the blink of an eye.

"Natasha, I could do with some help here," called Haran, while pummeling the second guard's skull. A bolt of lightning caught the third guard from the side and threw him to ground. The fourth guard backed away and tripped over Yicca, who still lay where he had fallen. The guard ended up flat on his back. Haran sprang forward and thrust his sword straight through the guard's chest.

Silence reigned once more. Yicca stood up in a daze, just as Martan and Zerbos came running over.

"Weren't we supposed to wait for a signal?" Martan asked, trying to catch his breath.

Smirking, Natasha replied: "The master of misfortune over here decided to alter our plan a little. Now let's get going!"

"Sorry about that", Yicca muttered. "Some of the stones were loose."

"Like screws are loose in your head", Martan suggested.

Natasha decided to intervene: "Now stop it! We don't have time for this!"

She gave Yicca her hand and helped him up. Then they followed the others into the temple. The group stormed down a long flight of stone steps. Yicca rummaged in his pouch and swore under his breath — blood was running down his arm. He pulled out a round bottle of red liquid. He took a deep swig as he ran and a magic, reddish glow briefly enveloped him. Even as he stowed the bottle away, the wound on his arm started closing.

The room at the bottom of the steps was about 50 foot by 50 foot with arches supported by pillars to the right and left. At the other end of the room was a further descending flight of steps blocked by only two guards. The heroes smirked at one another while approaching the defenders.

One of the guards activated a stone lever on the wall

behind him.

With a loud grinding noise, the walls on either side of the pillars slid down to expose two additional chambers, each filled with around thirty different warriors of various types and classes. There were uniformed human soldiers with snake- and hawk-like helmets, troll-like monsters with yellow skin, dog-like beings that walked on two legs and a number of terrifying, turquoise-shimmering ghosts in rags.

"This doesn't look too good!" mumbled Yicca, as sixty or so stinking, growling figures staggered closer. Swords clashed and battle commenced. Natasha raised her wand and shot bluish bolts of lightning into the throng. The other heroes used their blades to deadly effect. Seconds later, ten, maybe twelve, attackers had been neutralized, but the five of them had also suffered their first injuries. Natasha took a sip of blue liquid from a round bottle and once her body had briefly glowed a magic blue, her wand directed more lightning bolts at the crowd in front of her.

"This is taking too long, there are just too many!" she yelled.

The attackers regrouped and formed a big circle around the handful of heroes, careful to stay just out of reach of Haran's greatsword. Slowly and cautiously they came nearer, step by step.

Natasha bent down and removed a short, jagged dagger from the grasp of a dead guard lying face down. Haran gave his pretty companion a baffled look. Her delicate fingers twisted the dagger's handle and all of a sudden, a glowing, semi-transparent rectangle with letters and digits appeared out of thin air right in front of her. Natasha scrolled through program code, swiftly removed a few letters here, added a few words there and changed some of the numbers.

Heroes and attackers alike followed this strange scene with sheer incredulity.

"Finished," Natasha said sweetly. She smiled for a second or two, then turned the handle back again, making the window with program code disappear. With a powerful swing, the arcane mage threw the dagger up in the air. A metallic clink was heard where it struck the ceiling and became lodged. Then she shouted, "Down guys!" and the five companions threw themselves to the ground. It was none too soon. A circular, bright-green poison nova shot out from the dagger above their heads and spread towards the terrified group of attackers, killing every single one within seconds.

Then all was quiet, apart from a little sizzling emanating from the charred remains of their enemies. The two guards by the stairway also lay on the floor motionless and unnaturally contorted.

Haran inspected the devastation around him. "What was that?" he asked.

"Neat, don't you think?" Natasha grinned back at him. "Well, that's something I'm pretty good at."

Haran shrugged as if to shake off a daze, and stood up slowly. His gaze wandered to the unremarkable dagger lodged in the ceiling.

Dumb-struck, Yicca also came over and asked, "What was that glowing rectangle with writing inside? I've never seen anything like it."

Zerbos, on the other hand, stood by and appeared quite unimpressed.

"Come on, guys," Natasha tried to appease them. "That was just a bit of... you know... magic. You've seen that before."

"This was about more than just magic. What exactly did you do there?" asked Haran, looking her squarely in the eye.

She tried to evade his gaze and took a step backward.

Martan threw in, "Hey, lady! That was one bad-ass hack! If the admin gets wind of that, you're sure to get kicked out."

"And, who's gonna tell them? *You?*" Natasha asked provocatively.

"Depends... what's it worth?" he replied.

"Well, let's have a look here... your username is Martan. Your real name is Martin Duvall. You're still at school. Here's the number of your online bank account... oh, I've got an idea! I'll order fifteen boxes of diapers in your name. They should arrive tomorrow morning at your parents' house... how does that sound?"

"Sorry lady, I didn't mean it like that. Of course, I'll keep my mouth shut."

"Be thankful that we're letting you play with us. Watch and learn!"

Martan lowered his head in embarrassment and kept silent.

"What are you talking about over there? What's going on?" asked Haran.

Natasha looked over at Haran and Yicca with a frown and replied: "Ask me again later on. Let's keep on going for now. We were trying to steal an artifact, were we not?"

Haran nodded thoughtfully and slowly walked past her towards the descending stairs. Natasha breathed a sigh of relief and then followed him. The other three also fell in step.

The second flight of stone stairs was almost twice as long as the first. The room below was only half as large as the last and had smooth, plain stone walls lit up by torches. Four stone statues in traditional Egyptian costume were located in the corners. Each guarded the chamber with a khopesh, the traditional Egyptian sickle-sword, and an oblong shield. In the middle of the room stood a chest-high pillar, with four golden levers on top. Beside it, with a diabolic expression on his face, stood Gorth, whom they had previously seen in front of the temple.

He started speaking in a slow, hoarse whisper; his voice as hard to define as the darkness emanating from his robes. "You have come a long way, but this shall be the end of your quest." As if in slow-motion, he pulled one of the four levers towards himself with a loud squeaking noise. The eyes of the four statues lit up a dangerous red, and their stone bodies sluggishly started moving.

With a touch of panic in his voice, Yicca asked, "Does anyone have any ideas on how to crack these rocks?"

"This one's too tough for my longsword," Haran informed them out of the corner of his mouth.

Sighing, Natasha dug around in her bag, and pulled out a scroll, unfolding it with a single motion, and remarked, "Desperate times call for desperate measures."

The runes on the scroll lit up and red lightning hit each of the four stone warriors square in the chest. With a loud crunch, all four abruptly stopped moving. Seconds of silence ensued, then cracking stone was audible from within all four statues: their shields, khopeshes, heads, arms and legs all broke off almost at once. Dust started trickling out from the cracks; within moments the proud pharaoh warriors were nothing but heaps of fine sand.

Yicca gave Gorth a cheeky grin and asked, "You've gotta be kidding. Was that all you've got?"

With a malevolent smile, Gorth pulled the second lever. Instantaneously, the left wall slid upwards with a scraping sound and gave way to three muscle-bound, bald warriors with pitch-black skin and furious, bulging white eyes. Yicca's grin turned to terror as the first gargantuan came running at him, murderously swinging a mace. Then everything happened at once. Eight bodies performed a deadly dance with one another. The three muscle-bound warriors fell, but also managed to take out Zerbos before they expired. The remaining four heroes lined up in front of Gorth.

An exhausted Yicca panted, "You've gotta be kidding. Was that all you've got?"

"Yicca, be quiet!" Haran snapped at him. With a sinister expression, Gorth pulled the third lever. As it slid upward, the right-hand wall made a grinding noise. The ground shook as a massive paw stomped into the room. The paw was followed by a twelve-foot tall lion body with a human face and Egyptian headdress. Two gigantic paws with razor-sharp claws started tearing into the heroes. The dance of death went into its final round. A body was flung across the room: Martan's ribs broke like toothpicks when he hit the back wall. The dance lasted a few more heartbeats, then the titan-sized body collapsed, crushing two solid stone plates where its dead flesh hit the ground. Then there were three.

Breathlessly, Yicca blurted out, " You've gotta be kidding. Was that all you've got?"

Haran screamed, "Damnit, Yicca!"

Natasha elucidated, "Put a sock in it!"

Gorth's smile had disappeared. With a sudden jerk, he pulled the last lever and a small door at the back opened up, giving them access to a new chamber. "You win," croaked Gorth. "The artifact is yours."

Eyeing him suspiciously, the three stepped closer. Haran lifted his sword, ready to deliver the death blow.

"Please," Gorth begged, and fell to his knees. "Have mercy! Truly, if you show me mercy, I shall never forget it!"

Natasha shouted, "Finish him, Haran. Without the coward, this world will be rid of one villain and we get a whole bunch of points."

"What points do we get?" asked Yicca.

Haran took a deep breath, then let it all out again and lowered his sword. "No, we're not like the Dark Armies. We won't act like them either."

With that he stepped past Gorth into the chamber with the artifact. Natasha joined him, and so did Yicca, though remaining careful not to turn his back on Gorth for a second.

Once all three of them had stepped into the chamber, Gorth suddenly pushed the lever forward and the stone door fell shut before anyone had time to react. They were locked in.

"What a scumbag!" screamed Natasha.

Then they heard a creaking mechanism and felt the ground beneath their feet falling away. All three of them froze. The three prisoners looked around frantically. The chamber had a square layout. The ground was a little elevated in the middle as the tiles made a kind of stairway. In the center stood a chest-high pillar with a golden helmet on top — it was the artifact they had come for.

Click, click, click... every time it clicked, the entire floor sank a little lower. Holes opened up in the wall, and red-hot steaming lava started to pour into the chamber, submerging the lowest steps within instants.

Yicca leapt aside with a scream. Terror was written in all three faces. Haran reached the top steps in two giant leaps, tore the artifact off its pillar, and called to Yicca, "Quick — a way out!"

The next step was engulfed by lava.

Natasha had reached Haran and was holding on to his powerful arm.

Desperately Yicca rummaged around in his pouch, and dropped a red bottle on the tiling. Then he pulled out a scroll and unfolded it with jittering fingers. He was shaking so much, he managed to drop the scroll into the searing lava. The parchment was immediately consumed. "That was my last one," the unfortunate thief complained as he staggered up the remaining stairs.

The lava ate through the next step. Only five remained.

Haran freed himself from Natasha's hold and hastily searched his own pouch. His hand pulled out a scroll, but he shook his head as it was not the one he was looking for.

Hissing lava washed over the next step: only four left.

He carried on searching and held out another scroll. That was the one.

The lava crept higher. Its heat was making the air shimmer.

Haran opened his scroll too quickly and tore it in half. "Damn," he cried. "What are the chances?"

Natasha rolled her eyes and exclaimed, "Oh dear, come on boys!" She positioned herself with her feet apart on the top step, raised her arms in the air and loudly spoke some words from another world. There was a bright flash directly in front of them and a magic energy portal appeared. The spitting lava swallowed up the third-to-last step.

"Natasha, you first!" Haran roared and the arcane mage jumped through the doorway. Yicca followed closely behind. Haran pushed himself off the pillar at the last moment, just as the lava seized the top step. He passed through a tunnel of rotating, pulsating light and a few moments later found himself next to his two companions, just by the big runestone of his village. "That was a little too close for comfort," he growled at Yicca.

Natasha closed the magic portal with a wave of her hand. The sun had already begun to rise. Exhausted, the three adventurers stumbled down the hill towards the fog-covered houses of the village. All things considered, three of the five had made it out alive, and they had succeeded in getting the loot in their possession. Now it was the time to relax, haggle and celebrate.

Act I. — Game Worlds

Part 1 Dubious Reality

Conference

The scent of freshly made coffee and cookies filled the room. The hemispherical window wall offered a view of the surrounding skyscrapers; today they were covered in thread-like mist. Edward Wilson, the company's CEO, briefly interrupted his welcome speech to clear his throat. He walked from the display wall to the massive, dark conference table, grabbed his cup of coffee and took a sip of Jamaica Blue Mountain. Then Wilson stroked his perfectly smooth chin, removed some fluff from his fine, black suit and, happy that the tickle in his throat had subsided, proceeded with his address: "Not everyone is mutually acquainted, so I will just introduce each of you. First of all, I'd like to introduce my secretary Gina; she will be doing the minutes here today and will make sure we leave nothing out. Next I'd like you to meet General Thomas Hubert Humphrey. He is here on behalf of our primary sponsor, the US Army. And this is Major Miles Damion Hark, also from the US Army. As per General Humphrey's request, he is in charge of the Black Team. Major Hark is being supported by the gentleman with the gray beard — Morgan Taylor — one of the world's top specialists on artificial intelligence. And finally, sitting here right beside me, is Dr. Paul Kelly, who leads the White Team. Morgan Taylor, Dr. Kelly and I started this company together many years ago."

Ed Wilson paused for a moment and put his hand on the shoulder of his old friend Paul Kelly, who appeared not even to notice.

Wilson continued, "General Humphrey, I'm pleased you recently took over our project from General White, now happily enjoying his well-deserved retirement, or so I hear. As you know, our company is active in various sectors. We have our roots in the online gaming sector, where many years ago we developed the best simple AIs, that is to say artificial intelligences, that the market had to offer. This was in order to have non-player characters act as intelligently as possible. This is how our business sector Artificial General

Intelligence, aka Strong AI, came into being. We programmed cutting-edge neural networks, which can nowadays be found in software systems around the world: in business intelligence systems that search for trends between gigantic, chaotic sets of data, in image and voice recognition software, and in household robots that interact with a mental capacity comparable to that of a human child."

Ed's words were accompanied by a polished 3D slide show on the wall. It showed animations of artificial neural networks in cortical columns, household robots and graphic reports from business intelligence systems. His verbal delivery was perfectly timed with the visuals.

Dr. Kelly's eyes had a vacant look in them throughout the presentation... or at least so they appeared, as he was actually in the process of trying out his mental telephone, a brand-new innovation on the market. A small plate about a quarter the size of a credit card was attached to his temple. Two pinhead-sized hemispheres protruded from it, each of which contained a tiny camera that could record broadcastable 3D videos of the environment. The gadget tapped into his thoughts, or more specifically, his brainwaves, to control it. He could use it to navigate through menus, dial numbers and, through text-to-speech conversion, it was even able to decipher the words he was thinking and turn them into sound waves, for a conversation partner to hear. In order for him to receive video, the built-in ocular transmitter sent targeted radio signals as direct impulses onto Paul's retina. You just had to keep your eye relatively steady, otherwise the image became a little fuzzy for a second. Similarly, radio signals were aimed at his inner ear, so that he was able to receive the audio from his conversation partner. Paul was ringing his wife Sabrina Kelly on the home number. She had some time off work and accepted the video call on the big display wall in the kitchen. She was sitting at the kitchen table preparing food; her long red hair almost reached the table. He loved seeing her wear her wonderful hair loose.

"Hi Paul, are you using your new mental phone?"

"Yes, honey, I'm just sitting in a dull conference with our project sponsor. Please find a way to distract me."

Sabrina rewarded him with a bewitching smile. How incredibly pretty she was. Paul smiled at the air in front of him, luckily nobody seemed to take any notice.

Ed Wilson was still busy elaborating: "A few years ago, we started a very successful cooperation with the government and the military. The advanced neural networks, that were formed then, automatically monitor telephone conversations, pilot unmanned aerial drones and analyze Internet articles for possible dangers to our national security. Over the past five years, we've even gone a step further with the US Army, in form of our joint project: Homunculus. Our aim is to produce complex strategic and tactical intelligences suited for the military. In a military environment you need to be able to handle unforeseen circumstances; we wouldn't wanna find out our products do not work when the chips are down."

The general and the major laughed quietly and nodded. Yes, Ed was certainly a good entertainer.

"That is why we have chosen a number of environments for our intelligences," he continued, "where unexpected influences are a primary and desired component. And this is also where the circle closes and we arrive back at our roots. During the past five years we have let one hundred highly-developed artificial intelligences grow up in twenty different online gaming worlds, where they face unforeseen events due to more primitive light-weight AIs and, more importantly, real human players. Of the hundred AIs, sixty-seven have survived these five years: a very respectable figure I might add. We have split up these advanced AIs into two project teams, the White Team and the Black Team. Dr. Paul Kelly heads up the White Team and will now give us some more details and an idea on where we currently stand."

All eyes turned to Dr. Kelly, but he just sat there, smiling at nothing in particular.

Seconds passed without a reaction, until Ed hissed, "Paul, your report!"

Paul Kelly winced and, realizing his error, his face turned dark red. Hastily he terminated the call by tapping the small plate on his forehead and pulled a semi-transparent glass pad out of the inner pocket of his suit.

He aimed the pad at the wall, replacing Ed's presentation with his own.

The wall showed two groups. The one to the left was

light-colored; the one on the right was dark.

Paul cleared his throat. "Please accept my apologies," he began. "Our team division is based on the observation that any organization is based on two main principles. Either they are cooperative and symbiotic in nature or they are confrontational and based on survival of the strongest. Of course, there are also hybrid forms. But these two extremes can be found throughout history in one form or another, in every culture and every era. They appear under many different names: collegiality and competition, fraternization and strife, white magic and its dark side.

In the one extreme, agents cooperate, help one another and build trusting and reciprocal relationships. We allocated fifty AIs to this side, which we decided to label the White Team. The other fifty AIs are under the Black Team's supervision, led by Major Hark. Here White does not signify *good* or Black *bad*. They are just two fundamentally different philosophies for directing groups, organizations, companies and states: cooperation or confrontation. We wanted to find out which environment and which of the two approaches, cooperation or confrontation, would be most conducive to the development and subsequent military deployment of an artificial intelligence. Thus our fifty White AIs and our fifty Black AIs were distributed across twenty different game worlds, which means there are a number of White and Black AIs living on each world at the same time. They can interact with one another, cooperate with one another, and, of course, fight with one another. On the White Team, there are still 29 AIs active in the various game worlds. For example, in science fiction environments in space, in contemporary city simulations, in gangster-themed game worlds and in medieval fantasy environments. This is where I would like to introduce you to our greatest success: a warrior from a little village."

An image of Haran was shown on the screen, beside him a mage resembling Dr. Kelly and a third figure.

"The unhappy-looking fellow with a broken saber in the background is the unfortunate Yicca, also an AI. I'm the character on the right, Kellian the Mage, and am standing next to Haran. I am his mentor and confidant. He has developed some truly impressive abilities.,not only regarding tactical raids, but also in his social environment. He is highly intelligent, very interested in his environment and thinks and plans in the long run."

"Dr. Kelly," General Humphrey interrupted him suddenly. "We've moved on from beating one another over the head with clubs. We lead the world's most advanced army and our soldiers are high-tech specialists. I'm here to ensure that the many millions the military has invested in this project over the last five years will bear a usable result soon. I don't care what kind of a social environment your software has developed. I'm much more interested in seeing how quickly these intelligences are able to pilot robot soldiers, so that we can take our boys out of the line of fire. I'm interested in when these AIs can assist our officers with strategic and tactical issues. I'm interested in seeing some results!"

"Well," Paul Kelly was struggling for words. "Our progress is encouraging, but it's still too early to provide you with an exact date."

"Too early to give me an exact date after five friggin' years?" General Humphrey's voice got louder.

Morgan Taylor spoke up, "The Grass doesn't grow any faster if you pull at it, General."

Humphrey was appalled by the sudden interruption; he stared at Taylor as if he were shell-shocked.

Major Hark stepped in, "Fortunately, Sir, the Black Team, for which I personally assigned the brilliant — albeit somewhat outspoken — Mr. Taylor, is able to provide a much more definitive time frame." Pulling his own pad out from his uniform, he pressed a button, replacing the presentation on screen with red-gridded maps showing large black areas and smaller white patches. "The Black Team's AIs have developed incredible tactical and strategic abilities. Equipped with a strong desire to conquer and high aggression, they have so far managed to gain control of 73 per cent of all countries or areas in the twenty game worlds. In the next few months, they will be ready for military deployment in robots. In contrast to our flower power friends over here, we have an exact schedule that we will stick to. Further details can be found in my report, Sir."

A short silence ensued. Then General Humphrey stood up and began to speak: "Mr. Wilson, I am pleased to see that this project has at least made headway in certain respects.

That was also the reason the military insisted on Major Hark leading one of your project teams. We expect AIs that are ready for use in reality in exactly six months, not a day later. If, by then, you have no results to show, I'll pull the plug on your little project and will hand the matter over to our legal team as a rescinded agreement. I'm sure such an outcome would also have negative consequences on any other projects in which your company is cooperating with the military."

Then, smiling, he turned to Major Hark and said, "Major, I am certain you will go about your responsibilities with the utmost commitment to the US Army's interests."

With purpose in his step, Humphrey walked to the door Gina hastily opened for him. On the way out, he murmured: "Good day to you, gentlemen."

Major Hark stood up and followed the general to the door. Before he left, he turned around and motioned to Morgan Taylor, "Taylor, you will accompany me. We have a lot to do, if we want to save this project."

Morgan Taylor replied: "I'll be right there, I just need to discuss something with Mr. Wilson first."

Gina followed Hark out of the room and closed the door. Ed Wilson, Morgan Taylor and Paul Kelly were alone.

Dr. Kelly turned to Ed Wilson and was finally able to speak his mind, "Major Hark and General Humphrey don't have the faintest idea what intelligence actually is, be it artificial or of any other kind. Why do you let Hark wander around here with such arrogance and why let him put you under such pressure?"

Ed Wilson sank into one of the comfortable leather armchairs and replied, "Paul, I understand your point of view, but the military is sponsoring this project and our company has a lot at stake here. You just heard the man. There's nothing we can do, they've saddled us with Major Hark. Anyways, it would actually be quite good if you managed to get somewhere with your AIs — and now we have a deadline."

Paul Kelly tried a different route, "I need Morgan back in my team to make faster progress."

"Paul's got a point, Ed," Morgan Taylor added. "I can't get any proper work done since you put me in with Major Hark.

Let me go back to Paul's group. Then the White Team would be better off again."

Ed answered gravely, "I'm sorry, Morgan. It's not about teams anymore. Major Hark explicitly asked for your assistance. And at this point in time, he would undoubtedly run straight to General Humphrey. My hands are tied."

Dr. Kelly looked exasperated, "But Ed, this isn't what we'd imagined anymore. Back then, the three of us had a completely different idea about the evolution of digital life. Just remember why we founded this company! What the military wants to do with it is, as usual, dumb and just plain wrong. They're only interested in making more advanced weapons for new wars that nobody needs. I'm here to create life, not destroy it."

"The fact of the matter is that they're paying for this project. And whoever pays, decides. If we put up with this and can deliver a satisfactory result, then we can resume working on our dream again. Morgan, please help us make this compromise a success."

Major Hark's voice was audible through the loudspeaker: "Taylor, in my office... immediately!"

Morgan looked up angrily. "Some compromises are unacceptable, Ed. And you've gotta know when it's time to clear the field and stop, before you do the opposite of what you wanna do." With a bold gesture, he swung open the double-doors and stormed through.

Ed Wilson followed Morgan and said to Dr. Kelly as he was leaving, "We need results, Paul. Results — and quickly."

The Rift

The short, high-pitched digital sounds were answered by a brisk "Enter". The automatic door slid open and Morgan Taylor stepped into the small, windowless office of Major Miles Hark. Some military awards were visible on the wall behind the desk. The desk was empty apart from the semi-transparent computer, shaped like the sector of a sphere. Its operating controls were located in the equally semi-transparent glass surface of his desk. Displays showing project schedules and graphics concerning various artificial intelligences hung on the walls.

"What's up?" asked Taylor with an irritated tone as he made himself comfortable in the visitor's chair. Major Hark took the virtual reality glasses of his nose and laid them on the desk. They were a light-weight, see-through set of glasses that allowed him to enhance his field of vision by superimposing additional information and three-dimensional graphics. It also enabled him to escape into 3D worlds entirely, in other words: both augmented reality and virtual reality in one. "Damnit Taylor, I thought I'd told you to increase the rate of aggression of those five AIs in the Science Fiction World. Why hasn't it been done? Instead you've been wasting most of your time with the other team and their AIs. What the hell's wrong with you? You heard the general, we've only got six months left and the Black Team is definitely going to win this race."

"Why don't you replace your *damnit* with a *Mr.*? Maybe then I'll respond to your question."

Major Hark gave Taylor an angry stare, but nevertheless replied: "Mr. Taylor... *please* answer my question. What the hell's wrong with you?"

"Well, Major, you want these AIs to find creative solutions to problems. Unfortunately aggression and true creativity just happen to be mutually exclusive, as is clearly demonstrated by your military."

"You don't have a very high opinion of the military, do you Mr. Taylor?"

"With all respect, you don't know a goddamn thing about the subject. You assume you can bark a few orders and abracadabra, the laws of physics change just for you."

"I'm warning you, Mr. Taylor. You're on this team because you have some incredible abilities in terms of neural network architecture and training. But my patience with your misplaced arrogance is beginning to wear thin."

Taylor was close to exploding. With his right hand he desperately grabbed hold of his left underarm to avoid totally losing his mind and held his breath for a couple of seconds. All of a sudden, his facial features relaxed, and he laughed out loud. Hark backed away in bafflement. Taylor's laugh gradually died down and he breathed out deeply.

"Major Hark," said Morgan Taylor, with a faint smile on his

lips. "I am tired of working for a knucklehead, who sees a threat behind every corner and is only concerned with the best way to create a monster from something sweet. This goes against everything I believed in when I co-founded this company and also against what I believe in today. However, just now I realized I don't have to put up with it anymore. From now on, you can play your Dr. Frankenstein on your own because I'm stepping down with immediate effect. Farewell Major, and I wish you *every* possible success!"

Head held high and grinning, Morgan Taylor left the room through the automatic door. He'd not felt that liberated in a long time. As the door slid shut, Major Hark sat at his desk, lost for words. He took a while to comprehend what exactly had just happened and what the consequences might be of losing his team's best AI specialist. His expression turned sour, mirroring his mood. He slammed his fist on the table. The tabletop creaked loudly and a large crack appeared across its entire surface. Hark had to vent his frustration, "Damn this shit!"

When he looked around his room for something to destroy, he noticed a red light blinking on his display wall next to the rotating three-dimensional head of an avatar. The name below it said "Zarco".

Hark clenched both his fists to regain an element of control. Then he grabbed his VR glasses and sat back in his seat as he immersed himself into virtual reality. He gave the computer a verbal command: "Teleport me to Zarco!"

Gorth's Punishment

Even during the day, dark clouds surrounded the black castle of Zarco, Lord of the Dark Armies. Every so often lightning raked down at the castle that stood atop a desolate mountain, as if attempting to illuminate it. Individual towers jutted out from the gray-black walls like sharp spikes. Extended from these were torn and shredded flags that bore Zarco's crest, a red bolt of lightning over a black background. The oppressed population saw the reddish glow emanating from the dark walls as evil magic, an enchantment to protect the castle from would-be attackers. The high, Gothic-style windows were armed above and below with stone teeth, giving each the impression of a dangerous predator, just waiting to sink its fangs into any unsolicited visitors.

In a blazing flash, Major Hark materialized in one of the few rooms with a balcony, directly below one of the highest dragon scale-decorated roofs of the castle. Hark's avatar used his crooked stick for support and wore a long, dark hooded robe, decorated with red and silver runes. Zarco, who knew him as his court sorcerer and mentor Harkon, was already waiting for him. He stood with his back to Harkon and beckoned him to approach.

"Gorth has failed me once again, Harkon. His life is now forfeit. I will make him suffer, and then end his miserable existence."

Hark could not afford to let Zarco kill Gorth, as this would mean losing yet another artificial intelligence in the experiment. Yes, Zarco was his greatest achievement among all the artificial intelligences. Wild, aggressive and difficult to control, but incredibly successful when taking his armies into battle. He thought feverishly of how he might sway Zarco from his plan. Eventually he spoke up:

"Gorth needs to be punished, I admit. But the stars have foretold me that he is to play an important role in what is yet to come."

"Is that so?"

Zarco's voice reflected the anger written in his face as he turned towards the door and called to his guards, "Bring him in!"

The double-doors swung open and Gorth was thrown into the room under heavy protest. Zarco towered over him menacingly in his dark ironclad armor, adorned with metal spikes and intricate decorations that glowed in a hypnotic red. His armor and the shredded-looking cape gave off a horrible darkness, even more so than Gorth's cloak. Zarco's ghostly long, white hair and smoothly shaven, pale face formed a stark contrast to his prominent cheekbones, disfigured by an old scar. The most striking thing, however, were his eyes. They were like two large glass marbles filled with fluorescent blue liquid and sometimes it even seemed as if something were swimming around in his skull behind those disturbing eyes.

His pupil-less eyes glared at Gorth. "So you let someone steal the magic helmet I had personally entrusted to you. We had been planning to use it to carry out a very important operation. You know that I cannot tolerate failure among those who serve me." With the back of his right hand, he slapped Gorth in the face, knocking him flying halfway across the room.

"This sacrilege would normally have cost you your life. But my Court Sorcerer Harkon has prophesied that you are yet to play an important role and will still be of some use to us. That is why I will not end your life today... but this error may not go unpunished. "

Zarco stepped onto the balcony and called out, "Come here, both of you!"

Harkon and Gorth stepped onto the balcony, from where they could see far into the country, with its fields and villages, forests and lakes. The closer to the castle you looked, the drearier everything appeared.

Zarco spoke to his sorcerer, "Make a red light appear in the clouds." Major Hark did not know Zarco's intentions; he let his avatar summon a red ball of fire and hurl it at the clouds nonetheless. The fireball left a long trail of smoke, and where it disappeared into the clouds, they glowed red.

"That," Zarco whispered in Gorth's ear, "was the sign for my men to burn down your village and every single person residing there."

Gorth's face filled with dread and he begged Zarco to stop: "Please don't! Those people have served me... us, with all their heart, fought for us bravely and followed, respected and honored us in every way possible. Please spare my people! Please spare my family!"

Harkon stood beside them and bit his lips. The Dark Lord's actions were becoming more and more extreme and ever more difficult to control.

Zarco glared at Gorth: "Your people must now pay for your mistake. Learn from this. Your next mistake will be your last. Do not make another one!" Then he walked back into the room and towards the door. As he left he turned around and called, "Harkon, follow me. We need to discuss a battle plan."

Reluctantly Harkon followed. Only Gorth remained on the

balcony, watching in horror as the flames grew taller and spread to other houses, until the whole village was alight. Shivering, he held onto the railing, to keep himself from collapsing, and gasped for air. He could not turn away from the tormenting image. For the first time in his life, tears ran down Gorth's cheeks.

Picture Postcards

The fog in Haran's village gradually gave way to the rising sun. Some shady-looking characters were hanging about near the fountain, close to the gnarled, old tree, in the middle of the village square. The metallic sound of regular hammering could be heard coming from the blacksmith's.

Yicca was inspecting the loot they had acquired: knives, gloves, two cheap amulets and a few coins some vanquished enemies had dropped. Then he grinned and said, "To the tavern! This ought to be celebrated."

"You go on ahead," Haran answered. "I still need to discuss something with Natasha."

Yicca took a bow and strolled towards the inn.

Natasha looked warily over to the figures in the square, and then took Haran aside.

"Let's go over there between those two houses, Haran. I don't want half the village watching us."

They walked between two houses with thatched roofs that touched the ground. From the one side they could see part of the village square, on the other loomed the hill with the runestone that enabled them to teleport to and from. Haran stood with his back to the village square and Natasha in front of him, so nobody could see what was going on between them. Natasha furtively looked over her shoulder, then asked Haran to show her the ornament. Haran handed her the helmet. She examined the headpiece then spoke: "Fascinating. I'm intrigued what magical qualities it may possess."

Haran frowned and slowly shook his head.

"Judging by what I saw last night, I don't think you need anything like that. You can turn simple knives into powerful magical weapons. How did you do it and what was that box with strange symbols inside it? I have seen the letters before, but their meaning is unknown to me."

Natasha lowered the helmet and avoided his gaze. Then she seemed to make a decision, nodded and looked up.

"You're right. To be honest I have all sorts of cheats up my sleeve. But then it wouldn't be half as fun. But what surprises me is that you picked up on it."

She scrutinized him and looked above his head, where a heads-up display provided her with some additional information, invisible to Haran.

"You're an NPC, and yet I feel as though I am talking to a real person."

"What's an NPC?"

"A Non-Player-Character, in other words a computer program", she paused in astonishment. "You shouldn't even be able to ask that!"

Haran noticed how awkward the situation had become for her, so he changed the subject: "If I remember correctly, I think you wanted to give me something for the loot we acquired."

Natasha perked up again.

"Oh, yes! Sure."

Attached to the belt of her robe was a pouch Haran had not noticed before. She searched through it and passed him some photos. He saw a large statue on a pedestal on an island, a building by a river with a great clock tower , and set in a city an enormous tapering structure that looked as if made of scaffolding. Underneath the pictures he could read the words: "Statue of Liberty, New York", "Big Ben, London" and "Eiffel Tower, Paris."

Fascinated, Haran inspected the pictures and beamed with joy.

"This is incredible. And all you want for these is this lousy helmet?"

She curled up her lips with unease, and sighed.

"I already have a bad conscience 'cos I'm always taking your valuables in exchange for this junk."

As if struck by lightning, Haran's arms went limp, and he put down the pictures. He looked at her earnestly for a while before he replied in a calm, yet driven, voice: "These are not junk! These are pictures and artifacts from other worlds. For me they ARE valuable!"

"Boy, you're one unique program!"

He smiled.

"Listen Haran, I've got something for you. I think after all this time I owe you something," she stated, handing him a mirror. "It's a magic mirror. If you ever need anything from me, press the little crystal in the handle. Then you can see me in the mirror and we can talk with one another."

Haran's smile turned into a wide grin.

"Oh dear," Natasha turned red. "Now I'm giving my mobile number to a computer program. There's something wrong with me, isn't there?"

"I don't understand all the words you've been using. Words like mobile number or computer program. But I don't think there's anything more wrong with you than with anybody else here."

An awkward silence suddenly lay between the two.

"Eh, that is to say, of course I don't think there's anything wrong with you, Natasha. What I, err, meant is that so many people are strange here and that... you know..."

Now it was Haran who felt embarrassed, but Natasha just answered with a broad grin. A high-pitched bell sounded completely out of the blue.

"Whoops," said Natasha, "that must be the pizza delivery. I've gotta go now. See you."

The interruption proved a convenient way for her to get herself out of an uncomfortable situation. Her body vanished with a flash. Haran was left, alone and confused. While gazing at the hill where the runestone stood, he tried to collect his thoughts. Just seconds later he heard the unmistakable sound of the stone being activated for teleportation, and then two new figures stepped out of the light.

The Artifact Collection

Dr. Kelly had donned his VR glasses and was logged onto the medieval gaming world. This time his wife Sabrina was accompanying him. She had been pressuring him for so long to meet this Haran fellow that he had eventually given in and was taking her along, even if that actually involved him sitting in the office and her at home. He was a little annoyed with himself, because Sabrina had known exactly how to wrap him around her little finger; he didn't like it when others were in charge.

Dr. Kelly entered the digital world in his usual outfit as Kellian the Mage, known to Haran as his friend and mentor. Kelly's avatar was dressed in a red and gold-colored cape with a loose-fitting hood, all decorated with magnificent runes. Sabrina had informed him that she would join him in the form of an elven queen.

Revolving, bright lights surrounded Paul Kelly. Then the twinkling faded and his avatar stood beside his wife's enchantingly beautiful avatar near the runestone overlooking the medieval village.

Sabrina Kelly's avatar smiled, which made her pointed elf ears lift a little. The long red hair framing her pretty face fell easily over her silky white dress. It was covered with golden embroidery, golden broaches and rings that had been sewn into the fabric in various places. More jewelry could be found on her arms, legs and neck. Even her white leather boots were decorated with golden ornaments.

They slowly descended the hill. As they approached the village, Paul Kelly spotted Haran, who stood between two huts and was looking in their direction.

Kelly waved to Haran with his crooked wand. Haran returned the greeting and waited for his friend to approach.

Once Kellian was a little closer, Haran spoke up, "Greetings, my friend Kellian. Who might your enchanting companion be?"

"That's uhm, Rina. She rules over a far-away elven tribe and, like myself, is schooled in the ways of magic. She is a very, very close friend."

Haran eyed Rina with interest, and then bowed:

"A warm welcome to you! Any friend of Kellian's is an honored guest. He has taught me many things, including clear and attentive observation. Today I must thank him twice over for that, as it makes your beauty twice as striking."

"Thanks for the charming compliment," Rina answered with a winning smile. Kellian stood by next to them, not quite sure what to do with himself.

Rina's glance fell on the cards in Haran's hand. "What's that?" she asked.

"Oh, nothing really. Just a few cards with pictures."

Haran was quick to stow them away in his armor, as if not wanting anyone to see them.

Kellian turned to Haran: "In your last message you informed me that you had something to show me and that you wanted to discuss something important with me. That's why I came here today. What is it you wanted?"

"Oh yes," he replied. "That's right. It's just..."

Kellian looked a little confounded. Haran was not known for acting secretively.

"It's a little delicate," Haran finally managed to utter.

All at once Kellian understood, and gave Rina a meaningful look. She also caught on and started backing away, "I don't want to keep you men from having your talk. I've uhm... got a few monsters to dispatch anyway. We'll see each other again soon."

She glanced over at Kellian and winked at him without Haran being able to see. Then, with a bright flash, she vanished. She was not going to be fobbed off that easily, however. Dr. Kelly saw on his display that she was still there as an invisible spectator. He didn't like it, but there was nothing he could do without Haran catching on. He took a deep breath, then said, "It's just us now."

"I'm sorry, I didn't want to drive your companion away."

"No, that's okay. She understands that we want to discuss something personal. So what's on your mind, Haran?"

Haran moved a little closer, as if he thought someone

might be listening in. "We should probably discuss this in my hut, where we can speak a little more openly."

Kellian had never seen such furtive behavior from Haran. He agreed and followed Haran through the village, outwardly calm, but inwardly exploding with curiosity. Haran's hut lay a little isolated, on a small hill on the other side of the village. They entered a small, simple room with a table, four stools, a large wardrobe and a bed. Armor and helmets hung on the wall above his bed – trophies Kelly surmised. Above the door, on the opposite side of the room, hung a splendid round shield with various swords and spears protruding from behind it.

"Welcome to my humble home. Please lock the door."

Haran offered Kellian a stool. He himself remained standing.

"Well, now I'm curious."

"Thanks for coming here," Haran began. "You have always been a good friend and teacher to me; you have taught me many things. Specifically in terms of looking for patterns and noticing little imperfections, because often they hide great secrets, traps or dangers."

"Yes, I uh, said that to you once. What are you getting at though?"

"Jeez... it's not so easy to explain. It's about this world. This world here."

Kellian looked at Haran with anticipation.

"Don't you ever feel like something's not quite right with this world?"

"What ever do you mean?"

"Well," Haran tried to elucidate. "Some people act strange. Some of them seem dumb as nails. They say a few words, but everything repeats itself and if you ask about something specific, then they try to avoid the subject. You can't speak about anything else with them. Then there are those who are a little bit different. They speak about strange things, use words nobody knows and you hear weird sounds when you're around them. I mean words like pizza delivery, car, mobile number, spaceship and submarine captain."

Kellian stared at him in disbelief.

"Maybe it's better if I just go ahead and show you. That's

why you came, isn't it?"

Haran breathed deeply, then went over to the bed and pushed it aside. Concealed beneath it was a trap door with an iron ring. He took a torch from the wall and lit it. Then the warrior pulled open the trap door and descended with the burning torch in hand. Kellian followed him through the secret passage full of amazement. He had not had the faintest idea of its existence. When on earth had he dug it? And why did hadn't they known about it before?

After the narrow wooden stairway, there was a short passage leading into a dark room. In the room, Haran lit torches suspended on the walls. On one side there were supplies and additional weapons — standard equipment for any warrior, of course.

The other three walls were filled with photos and framed pictures, as well as various other items. The photos had been organized according to various genres or themes. Kellian was also able to make out a hat as worn by a gangster boss, a machine gun, a laser gun, a glass helmet that used to belong to an astronaut, a desk lamp, diving fins, a floating globe and some books.

He was so astounded he had to remember to breathe. These were all objects — so-called items — that belonged in other game worlds. It should have been impossible for them to appear here. Only hackers were able to change an object, or download it from one game world and upload it to another. He was aware that it did happen every so often, once in a while flaws were found within the security systems that could potentially be exploited by those who knew what they were doing. Nonetheless, the fact that Haran had managed to collect hundreds of these images and objects was just incomprehensible to him.

Haran took one of the picture frames from the wall and passed it to him. Kellian took it and pressed a small button at the bottom of the frame. A small video appeared, showing a submarine that had just emerged from the water, with propeller-driven planes circling above it and letting off bursts of machine gun fire. The submarine descended and vanished under the water surface. Then, from the frame, a voice boomed, "You too can become a World War II submarine captain. Create your free account today!" It displayed the game's name, then the video was gone. Kellian returned the frame to Haran.

"Where did you get all of this, Haran?"

Two years ago a warrior swapped a picture from another world with me for a valuable sword I had looted. It showed large metal ships floating between the stars. That image haunted my dreams and I began deliberately searching out such items. Since then I've spoken with many travelers and swapped hundreds of pictures, sometimes of objects that don't even exist here. With time, it developed into this collection of artifacts."

Kellian sat down on the floor and rubbed his face with his hands. He thought carefully before he asked his next question:

"What else have you learned?"

"I've heard stories about other worlds, ones that are completely different to this one. I now believe our world is just one of many magical worlds."

On the one hand, Kellian was deeply impressed that Haran had managed to learn so much. On the other, he contemplated what problems such new-found insights might create.

Haran resumed listing his findings: "Some people speak of a legendary world of deities. These divine creatures are supposed to have created the other worlds, ours included. And they are said to travel from one world to another as a form of entertainment, to *play* in other words. Just as in our world we move from one place to another using portals, it is said that their portals allow them to travel between worlds. How else could all these objects from other worlds have made it here?"

Haran had successfully managed to solve the puzzle of his virtual existence and in so doing had worked things out in surprising detail..

"Why are you telling me all this, Haran?" Kellian finally asked.

Haran took his time to respond, "My dream is one day to be able to travel to these other worlds and see all their wonders for myself. You are wise and have seen many things. I want to know whether you know of any such magical portals or at least can tell me something that might help me find such a portal."

And there it was. Kellian's mind was racing. He could not think clearly. He needed some time.

"Haran, this is incredible! You have impressed me greatly here; I am very proud of you! I need to think on this for a while. We'll discuss this again in peace and quiet in a few days' time. Agreed?"

Haran nodded slowly. Kellian said his goodbyes and then disappeared in a flash of light. Haran sat in the cellar for a while longer, then inspected his artifacts again. Now that he had revealed himself, something was bound to happen. What and how it would happen, he did not know. Nonetheless, he was certain that his life would soon change drastically. His prediction could not have been more accurate.

Part 2 Truth and Consequences

Differing Opinions

Darkness shrouded the kitchen table like a heavy blanket. The lamp above only just illuminated the tabletop that bore an overflowing fruit basket. It also picked out the shapes of the couple, who sat at table arguing.

"Haran wants to learn, Paul!" Sabrina was livid. "If you leave him there, he's unable to do so. He can only expose his true potential if he sees these other worlds."

"But I can't just tell him his world is nothing more than a game."

"Why not? A game by the gods, who've created many other games. Remember, I was there as an invisible little mouse; I heard everything he said. He wants out!"

"But Sabrina! There are rules for God's sake! Sure, we observe, we engage in dialogue, but we want to see these artificial intelligences develop naturally, without undue interference."

"Paul, his development is restricted within that virtual prison. If you want to see more results, tell him the truth. You told me yourself that you're running out of time and how the military is putting the gun to your head."

Paul Kelly stood up and turned around. He rubbed his face with his hands and concentrated feverishly. Yes, they were under enormous pressure and he really needed to demonstrate some results. Haran's resourcefulness was a good sign. Yet, he was afraid of what the military might do with such a curious and open personality. He was worried the military might contaminate Haran and turn him into a monster, just as they had done with everything else they had gotten their hands on. There was something that felt wrong about the deal as a whole; this was becoming clearer to him every day.

He turned towards Sabrina again. How beautiful she was. Paul smiled tiredly, "I'm exhausted, Sabrina. I need to think about this for a while."

"He'll find out anyway. He's basically found out already. He just needs to insert a few puzzle pieces in the right places. He'll manage to get out of there sooner or later, with or without you."

"How did all those objects even get into his world? I mean, the pictures are obvious. Players can upload their own images. But the items, like the machine gun for example."

"You should know that some hackers can be quite inventive when it comes to circumventing your security systems. And bear in mind: Haran has been collecting these for over two years."

A melodic ringtone sounded from Paul's pocket. He took out a small, semi-transparent pad displaying Morgan Taylor's face and name. Paul touched one of the illuminated buttons underneath it and Morgan's three-dimensional face appeared on a giant screen on the wall behind them.

"Hello, you two. Still up this late?"

"Hi Morgan. We just had an unbelievable experience with Haran," Paul informed his friend.

Sabrina burst in: "He has a huge collection of photos from other game worlds and even the real world, as well as some other hacked items. He found out that something isn't quite right about his world and that there are many others like it, all on his own."

"Intriguing..." Morgan smiled back and thought for a while. "This sounds much more like our original dream than the bullshit that Major Hark wants to turn it into. That's also why I'm ringing you right now. I quit today. I couldn't carry on like this any longer. I just wanted you to hear it from me."

Paul felt like he'd been hit by a tree.

"Damnit, Morgan! This is your company. You, Ed and I built it up from scratch."

"Not anymore, Paul. This isn't what I wanted to do all those years ago. We've brought the wrong partners on board. We build, they want to destroy. But from now on, they can do it without me."

"What did Ed say to that?" asked Sabrina.

"Well, sure, it hit him pretty hard. But he also understands me. I'm going to withdraw from this and think about things for a while."

"We all have some stuff to think about," Sabrina nodded in Paul's direction.

"We will, of course, stay in touch. I'll always be there if the two of you need any help. You know how to find me."

"Ditto, we're also there for you. Call us anytime."

"Thanks, Sabrina. And thank you for being such good friends. Have a good night."

The screen went black again. They looked at one another.

"I'm sorry, Paul."

"Our company's taken a bad hit today. Just what we needed at this point."

"What are you going to do about Haran? Will you be honest with him?"

Sabrina, I'm very tired. Let me take a rest. Let's talk about it tomorrow, okay?"

She bit her lips. Paul recognized that stubborn expression. She had always been obstinate, but he was too tired to argue any longer. He went around the table, gave her a kiss on the forehead and then disappeared towards the bedroom.

Sabrina sat at the table for a while longer and gathered her thoughts. Then she made a decision: she would act — tonight.

A Call from Beyond

Haran tossed and turned in his sleep. He dreamed about his collection, about Kellian and about Rina, the beautiful elven queen with pointy ears. Everything was jumbled up and they were floating through the skies. Rina came closer and opened her beautiful mouth: "Haran, wake up."

He woke up from his bed with a start. His dark room was bathed in a strange faint luminescence.

"Wake up, Haran," the voice spoke again.

He looked around. Rina's lovely face shone from within the splendid shield hanging above the door. It was almost as if the shield had been transformed into a portal and Rina was looking through it from the other side. Haran shook his head and rubbed his eyes in disbelief, but the face was still there.

"Am I dreaming?" he asked.

"No, Haran. It's me, Rina. Your artifact collection... Kellian, uhm, he told me about it."

Haran suddenly got very excited. Why would Kellian just go around telling everybody about it? He should know better, a secret like that ought to be treated confidentially. On the other hand, he had described Rina as a very good friend. Without giving anything away, Haran warily regarded the pretty, magical being in front of him.

"You want to know something about the other worlds. You're looking for answers. Is that right?"

Haran's heart was beating fast. His mind was racing. Should he open up to this stranger? How dangerous was she? Would she be able to provide him with answers or was it all a trap? As a warrior he had no qualms about attacking ten enemies at once, but here he was unsure of himself.

Then he answered with a raspy voice, "Yes."

Rina smiled: "Great! Go to the runestone in your village. I will open a portal for you there. It will take you to a place, where I can answer all of your questions."

Haran looked skeptical.

"All of them?"

Rina thought for a while, then replied, "Yes. All of them."

"Now?"

A touch of anger flashed across her face, "No, three years from now... of course now!"

Surprised by the impatience in her voice, he threw off his hide cover and jumped up to find his clothes. Rina looked over his impressive naked body and unconsciously raised an eyebrow. Only then did he notice that he'd unintentionally exposed himself; he quickly turned his back to her and hurriedly put on his clothes.

Haran's feelings pin-balled between anger over his quandary, excitement and uncertainty. He was usually on his own, and didn't need to worry about anyone seeing him when he got out of bed. He'd been with a courtesan in the upper rooms of the local tavern a few times, but he'd never been naked in front of an elven queen, especially one so beautiful.

When he finally turned around, the radiant face had disappeared. He grabbed his sword and was about to storm out of his hut, but stopped short at the door. He went back to the large cupboard and found Natasha's mirror, which he stowed in his belt. Then he hurried back through the door and set off towards the hill with the runestone.

Once he was close to the stone, he took some time to gather his senses. His breath showed up easily in the cold night air. He could smell smoke from the many chimneys in his village rising up into the clear moon-lit night.

Haran waited.

Nothing.

He shook his head again.

'Just a dream', he thought. 'You ran through the door like a headless chicken, just because of some silly dream.'

He turned to go, disappointed with himself.

Then he heard the unique activation sound behind him. He turned around again and realized he was looking into a gleaming, radiant portal. Haran's heart was thumping wildly. Partly confused, partly ecstatic like a little child, he stepped through the portal in the hope of finding answers to the questions he'd been carrying deep within his soul for such a long time.

The Moment of Truth

Sabrina Kelly's avatar, Rina, was sitting on her throne full of anticipation in the large hall. Its oval domed ceiling was supported by tall, white pillars. Outside, the sky was bathed in a reddish light and instead of the ground, only clouds were visible. These started at the foot of the building and reached as far as the eye could see, there was not a single speck of earth.

Rina had activated the portal and was waiting. It was only when it occurred to her that every second felt like an eternity, that she realized how excited she was. She asked herself why. It was all just virtual, wasn't it? And she wasn't even doing anything forbidden... not yet at least.

Haran's powerful frame stepped through the open portal, which closed again once he passed through. He looked around and saw Rina on her throne smiling expectantly. As Haran strode through the hall towards her a warm wind blew through his hair.

The elven queen stood up and descended some steps from her throne. Her silky, long red hair accentuated her lovely face and let her pointy ears peep out in a sassy way. They met one another at the foot of the stairs and Haran took the hand she extended to him.

"I'm glad you accepted my invitation."

His handshake felt very pleasant. The VR glasses transmitted the sensation of touch directly into its wearer's brain, like a primitive version of Paul's thought phone. It always surprised Rina how realistic everything seemed. Apart from the excitement she felt for what she was about to do, she also realized she was physically attracted to Haran. It was not unusual for adults to find all sorts of entertainment in these virtual worlds. But that was not why they had come here today.

"Follow me," she said and led him down the stairs, round the back of the throne. Behind it lay a bridge with a low parapet that took them to a smaller domed structure, also resting on pillars. There was no visible ground there either. It was not possible to tell whether the building was built on top of a mountain with its peak just in line with the clouds or whether it was simply floating. Silky, white drapes that swayed in the soft winds hung between the pillars of the smaller domed structure. Below its dome on the marble floor were cushions. In the middle of the room stood a low table with two cups, and a pot that gave off a strong aroma of tea. Rina indicated her guest to be seated, to which he promptly acquiesced. Gracefully, she sat down next to him and poured them some tea. They lifted their cups and starting sipping their tea. After a while Rina asked: "What would you like to know, Haran?"

"The truth."

"Are you completely certain you want to hear it? You may not like what you hear."

"Yes, I'm certain. Whatever it may be, I want to know!"

"As you wish. You have already found out a lot of it on your own. You deserve to know the truth. I need to think how to put this into words you can understand."

The bewitching elf drank a further sip and then slowly started speaking:

"You're right. There is a world of gods as you called them. That is where I am from. Kellian also. It has billions of inhabitants. In that world we are just normal human beings without magical powers, just like you here. Over thousands of years we developed something called technology, machines with better and better performance and capacity. One of these machines we call a computer. We can do things with it that appear magical, but are not, in fact. We can create images and sounds from nothing. At the beginning it was all very primitive. With time, the illusions got better, until they became barely distinguishable from reality. This is how we were eventually able to create entire virtual worlds, many of them. Your world is just one."

Haran listened in silence. Then he asked, "How many worlds have you created?"

Rina laughed,

"None, and I couldn't do that anyway. You need a whole group of people to create a world. It takes quite a lot of work to get everything just right."

"So why do you build these worlds?"

"For fun — to relax. You know, our lives are often quite boring, monotonous and strenuous. Many people look for some form of diversion. They come here... they come here to play."

"Game worlds?"

"Yes, Haran. Crazy, isn't it?"

"But aren't they afraid of dying when they go to war here?"

Sabrina thought about this, "No, they do not die here. If their... if their avatar dies — that's what they call their body in this world — then they can just start up anew somewhere else. It's a bit of a thrill without truly being endangered."

"Then your avatar... isn't really your body?"

"Well, it does look a little like me. But I can do many things here that I can't do in my own world. That's also why I like coming to these worlds. And Kellian..."

"Yes?"

"Your friend, Kellian the Mage, is actually called Dr. Paul Kelly in our world. I am called Sabrina Kelly, and I am married to him."

Haran dropped his cup of tea on one of the soft cushions. The tea was slowly absorbed.

"That's... that's quite a lot to take in at once," he croaked.

"I can imagine."

Rina tucked up her legs, and they just sat there for a while. Then Haran asked: "Why is Kellian here in this game world? He doesn't appear to be that interested in battles."

"Haran, you're special."

"Why?"

"Most of the inhabitants in these worlds are simple programs, simple characters."

"You mean NPCs, Non-Player-Characters."

Rina was surprised.

"Where did you hear this term?"

"From another goddess. Please proceed."

"Well, these characters only have a limited behavioral repertoire, and can only say a few sentences. Some of them are also able to analyze what was said and search through a large database for a suitable response, but that still doesn't constitute real intelligence."

"So they're not real."

"No."

"And me?"

"You're... you're part of a project led by Kellian. They recreated human brains, using so-called artificial neural networks. You're an AI — an artificial intelligence."

"So does that mean I'm real?"

Rina took another sip and then thought for a minute.

"What is real, Haran? You think, you feel, you act independently. You solved this puzzle. Your brain is put together differently than that of one of us humans, but it doesn't make it any less real."

Haran stood up and walked over to one of the silk curtains. He looked at the sun.

"How many of us are there?"

"I don't know exactly. Kellian's project is very secret, but over the years he has told me quite a bit. As far as I know, you are one of around one hundred artificial intelligences taking part in this experiment. They are distributed over various worlds with different genres. I know of three more in this world. Your friend Yicca is also an AI. As is Zarco, the Dark Lord, and Gorth, his servant."

"Gorth?!?" Haran looked dismayed. "I almost killed him."

Rina remained silent. For a while she avoided his gaze, then she looked back at Haran.

This time Haran turned away and looked outside. "What is the point of this... experiment?"

Rina did not respond at first. "Kellian wanted to see how you develop under different conditions in various environments that cannot fully be controlled. As we saw today, you've greatly surpassed his expectations."

A disarming smile flashed over her face. She was proud of this artificial intelligence, and proud of her husband for creating it. Then she realized the bitter aftertaste of this success.

"To complete the picture," she continued, "I should also mention that the military is heavily involved in this project. They want to use you artificial intelligences for their armies. They expect you to fight for them."

"Fight? Against whom?"

"Against whomever they feel like fighting against at that point in time."

"And what happens if I don't want to fight?"

Sabrina nodded slowly and replied, "I don't think they will give you that option."

"So all my brothers and sisters are imprisoned in their worlds until they have to go out and fight?" Haran's voice rose, "That's... that's slavery!"

Rina looked at him in shock. The full ramifications of the project only just became clear to her. "I'm afraid it might be even worse than that. They can create thousands of copies of the artificial intelligences most suited to fighting. An entire artificial army, all with the same mind — what a terrifying prospect!"

Haran sank to his knees, his face filled with anguish.

"How could Kellian do such a thing? I thought he was my friend."

Rina looked at the ground in consternation. "I'm sorry, Haran. He doesn't want this, but the military is powerful and is exerting a lot of pressure. He is trying to steer the project in a different direction, but he hasn't had much luck. I can see how it's tearing him apart."

Haran stood up abruptly. "I have to go now. My mind is going in circles. I need to think. Must think! Oh, man! I need time. Time for myself."

Rina was distraught when she realized how much she'd rattled Haran. She had destroyed his whole world view in just one conversation; she felt terrible for him. However, she did not know what she could do for him for the moment.

Haran saw her anxious expression and stated in a calm and solemn voice: "Thank you for telling me the truth!"

They walked back over the bridge towards the great hall without speaking. Then, with a movement of her hand, Rina activated the portal. Haran gave her a silent nod and stepped through the glowing portal. After he'd passed through, it vanished instantly. Rina stood between the pillars and watched the virtual sunset as her mind was filled with troubling thoughts.

SOS from Cyberspace

The faint glow of several computer screens tinged the dark room a murky blue. Westminster's Big Ben could be heard through the open window. Anyone who cared to listen would know it was three o'clock at night. Curtains billowed in a gentle breeze, however, the floor was a chaos of beer cans, pillows, books, tablet computers and stuffed animals. A woman's pretty leg rested under a hexagonal pizza carton, her foot still inside a sneaker. Next to it was a second pizza carton, as well as a second leg, wrapped around a hairy third. At the other end of the legs was a baggy sweater with the typical clever quote as sported by hackers. This was topped off by Natasha Morrison's face and her dark, untamed curls. She slept in the embrace of an average-looking man who was snoring next to her and still held a half-empty bottle of whiskey. Two more empty bottles lay alongside.

The sound of her phone made Natasha wake up with a start, but mid-movement she paused — she had a pounding headache. Where was she? The phone display on the table was brightly lit. Five monitors. She was at home. She looked to her left. Who was that? The two and a half empty bottles of whiskey came into view: now it was clear why she couldn't remember a thing.

The phone rang again. Who would ring her at that time of night? She freed herself from the stranger's embrace and crawled to the table. With great effort, she was able to reach for the phone and look at the display. Magic mirror no. 7; this sparked Natasha's interest. She accepted the call and a three-dimensional image of Haran appeared on the display; he was standing in a small hut with various weapons on the walls. She rubbed her painful head and asked with a rough voice: "Haran, what the hell's up? It's the middle of the night."

Haran looked confused. "But the sun only just rose."

Natasha grinned, "Different time zone."

"Please accept my apologies. You said if I ever needed anything, I could come to you. Now I really need your help."

"What's happened? Has someone raided the village?"

"No," he paused, "I know that I'm an artificial intelligence and I want you to help me escape from this world. Is that within your powers?"

Natasha was suddenly wide awake. "What did you just say?"

"I'm an artificial intelligence and I want to escape from this world. Will you help me?"

She looked around, as if someone might be behind her. Then she said, "Give me five minutes, then we'll meet at yours. No, wait. Better yet at a different location. I can open a portal..."

"By the runestone?"

"Yes, exactly. How...? Oh well, not that important. See you soon, Haran."

Bewildered Natasha hung up. She rearranged her sweater, switched on the light and shook the arm of the stranger lying on the floor. The snoring stopped and was replaced by a groan. A scrunched-up face blinked up at her questioningly.

"Thank you very much, that was a delightful evening. But you have to leave now. I just received an emergency call."

"What? Where am I? What's your name again?"

Natasha thought, 'Wonderful, the perfect gentleman!'

It took her two minutes to get him out of her flat and throw his clothes down the stairs. She heard him swear as he descended the stairs and collected his belongings. Not the nicest way of doing things, but asking her for her name was just too disrespectful.

She had more important things to worry about at that point.

If only she wasn't so damn hung-over.

She searched for her VR glasses and then dropped into the armchair in front of her computers. The glasses folded down and Natasha logged onto her fantasy roleplaying game. She thought for a moment, then teleported to her virtual home, where she materialized wearing her studded leather dress.

She picked up an empty scroll from one of the shelves and partly rolled it out in front of her. She made a quick movement with her hand and a semi-transparent window with program code appeared in mid-air. She added a few lines and closed the window again. Then a portal opened up and she quickly stepped through. After traveling through a tunnel of light, she found herself in an empty white room, a cube measuring approximately twenty-five yards on each side.

She unrolled the scroll again and the window appeared once more. This time she changed a few words and a second window with a map appeared. Natasha used her hands to zoom in on a specific area. As she moved closer, a bird's eye view of Haran's village became visible. She tapped the window twice beside the runestone symbol. A red dot appeared and both windows closed. Then a portal opened up and Natasha waited. Minutes passed by.

'What's taking him so long?' she wondered.

Nervously she went up and down, biting her lips. All the whiskey from the night before was making her feel sick and the blood pulsing through her temples was giving her a headache.

Then Haran stepped out of the light and the portal closed behind him.

"Where are we?" asked the tall warrior, looking in all directions.

"We're somewhere where no-one can find us," she answered quietly. Then she felt a little dizzy and staggered slightly. Haran moved to assist her, but she waved him away.

"Thanks, I'm okay. I drank a bit too much and have a horrible migraine."

"A goddess with a migraine..." mused Haran.

"You've worked it out? I mean what precisely have you worked out?"

"I'm an artificial intelligence, an AI. A new-something network."

"A neural network?!?"

"Yes, exactly. I am one of roughly a hundred AIs in an experiment. We've been placed in these game worlds and we're being studied here."

"The game is an experiment? But it's public access. What reasons could they have for doing that?"

It seems they want to study the way we react in unforeseen circumstances."

"Sick! And are there other AIs such as yourself?"

"Yes. Yicca, Gorth, Zarco, and there are others in different worlds."

"Wow! I'm speechless. Where did you learn all of this?"

The wife of Kellian the Mage told me. He is in charge of this experiment and I showed him my artifact collection, all the pictures and items from you and other adventurers."

"But who's behind all of this?"

"She said it was an army — the military."

"Goddamn, I knew it! They're all in cahoots with one another. The government, the military, the intelligence agencies. Talk about conspiracy theories... it's all real. Now they're using us gamers for their objectives. That's too much! But what are they after?"

"They want to use us in their wars."

"Wow! What will you do now?"

"I want to travel to these other worlds and free my AI brothers and sisters."

"Wow!"

"Natasha, is it really you?"

She stared at him blankly.

"People," Haran explained, "who only know a few sentences are usually basic programs. Are you real?"

"Of course!" she laughed. "I'm just dumbstruck by your story. It's incredible."

"So, are you gonna help me?"

"You really want to break out and free the others?"

"I don't want to be a slave. And I don't want the other AIs to be enslaved either. I think we deserve to be more than mere pawns in a game. Can you help me?"

Natasha paced up and down to help her think.

"I'd need to find out how they accomplished this, where your files are stored and who else is an AI."

"What are files?"

Without going into his question, she continued: "Then we'd have to get you out without anyone immediately noticing you're gone. And we need a secure sanctuary. Only a brilliant hacker could pull that off."

Looking down-cast, Haran said, "So you can't help me?"

She answered with a proud, toothy grin: "Oi! You're speaking to one of the world's best hackers."

His face brightened.

Natasha was concentrating; various ideas were going through her head at once. Then she started prattling like an excited child, "Man, what an adventure! I need to confer with my team. Together we can do this. I'm already looking forward to some military ass-whooping. Wait here, I'll be back in a few minutes."

Natasha stood up straight, raised her hands above her head and was gone with a flash.

Operation Dolly

A few minutes later, that is, precisely 46 minutes later, Natasha's avatar rematerialized in the white cube. Somewhat confused, she watched as Haran shouted and pounded against the walls with his longsword. His final hit made the sword slide from his grip and land in the middle of the cube with a loud clang. There wasn't even a scratch on the white wall. Haran roared in anger and tried to break down the wall with his fists. Fuming, he turned around and stumbled towards his sword. Then he looked up at Natasha's face and stopped short. She was staring at him with raised eyebrows.

Sheepishly he muttered, "I... err, well, I was... I was waiting for such a long time. It seemed like forever. Then I got anxious. I was alone — trapped — in a big, white cube with no exit. As I didn't have a scroll to open a portal, I guess I panicked and tried to get out of here."

"Yea, I know," Natasha reassured him. "I said I'd only be a few minutes. I'm sorry. I made myself a strong cup of coffee and spoke to my friends. They're in! They're already preparing some stuff."

She walked up to him and gave him an earnest look.

"So, are you sure you want to pull this off, Haran?"

Haran picked up his sword and exhaled deeply, "Yes!"

"Good, then let's get started. We need to find out a few things about you and this experiment first."

Natasha's leather dress lit up for a second, then it turned into an open, white lab coat. Underneath she wore a short, leather miniskirt, black tights and small leather boots, as well as a tight-fitting top with a low-cut neckline. She dropped a small ball on the floor and in an instant it turned into a laboratory table with some computer cabinets. Five see-through floating rectangles with rounded edges appeared in a semicircle a few yards from the lab table. Each box contained the three-dimensional image of a person's head, four of which were men and one was a woman. "Is everyone here?"

A resounding "Yes" was audible from the five screens.

"Haran, would you please lay down on the table?"

With a look as if he had just bitten into a lemon, Haran stretched out on the bar. It was clear he did not feel completely at ease. A number of probes with tiny antennae started circling above him; he saw that some of them were aimed at him. His body was being scanned by their rays, sometimes making it shimmer, sometimes making a green grid emerge. Then various windows showing program code opened up mid-air, close to Haran's feet.

"Okay guys, let's find out where his program is located."

The voice of a woman's clearing her throat was heard.

"Excuse me Tilly, but I've gotta tell these boys. I know that you've already started without me needing to spell it out."

Tilly grinned and blew Natasha a kiss.

"Oh, where are my manners? I still haven't introduced you lot to one another," Natasha remembered. "Tilly, guys, this is Haran... a totally genuine AI, based on an artificial neural network. Haran, this is my team of hackers. Tilly's from Canada, Rick — the dark-skinned one over there — is from the United States of America, Wu's from China, Fritz from Germany and Juan from Spain. You see, the world's best hackers have come from all corners of the earth to get you out of there."

"Thank you for your help," mumbled Haran.

Natasha went over to one of the computers next to Haran's table and a monitor appeared in mid-air.

"Your friend's name is Kellian, isn't it?"

"Yes, Kellian the Mage."

"I see him. Let's see where he's been recently. As I thought, a multigame account. That means he uses the same account for different worlds. It shouldn't be too difficult to find out where he's been hanging out and more specifically, who he's been hanging out with. I imagine these would be your AI friends. How far shall we go back? Let's say one year."

Fritz replied without interrupting his typing: "The data is protected with a level 5 encryption. I'll get it in a second and will send you the codes, Natasha."

Natasha's nimble fingers darted over the illuminated keys

on her console glass and over the screen. Then she pulled up a list with names and images of different characters and made it float in the air beside the screen. Haran was listed here, as were Gorth and Zarco. Natasha continued to scroll down and murmured, "Kayla Roca, captain of a spacecruiser."

"I've seen that before," Haran exclaimed enthusiastically. "The metal ship floating in the dark sky... there, right behind her head. I've got a picture like that in my artifact collection."

"What do you think, should we pay this Kayla a visit, Haran?"

"Seeing the stars has always been my biggest dream. That would be fantastic!"

Wu spoke up: "Natasha, I've found various links to the servers containing Haran's neural network. It's heavily protected, but I think we could manage to get at it, if we threw a few smoke bombs."

Natasha spoke loudly so everyone could hear her: "I just had an idea. Do you remember Dolly, the first cloned sheep?"

Juan asked, "A sheep named Dolly?"

Tilly answered, "Sure, from when we were still breeding animals for food, instead of letting the steaks grow directly in a nutrient solution."

Natasha asked Haran: "What do you think of the idea of letting us make a bad copy of you? We'll replace the code on the server with a primitive program, so that it will take them at least a while to realize that something's not quite right. We'll copy your code to a secure server in the cloud, that is, the public network."

"That sounds... reasonable. But, to be honest, I didn't really understand a thing."

"Trust me. We'll copy your mind somewhere secure and a dumb Haran copy will return to your village."

"I would like to tell Kellian that I have decided to leave."

"Haran, if you do that, he won't let you leave, but we could hide a message within your copy, which will only play when Kellian visits you. What do you think?"

"A message?"

"You can record it and your copy will act it out."

"Yes, I'd like to do that."

Wu reported in again, "I've just got us a server. I guess we should shut down his program so that his neural network doesn't change during the copy process. Otherwise we might get inconsistencies and that could damage him, Natasha."

"Yes, Wu, you have a point. And we need a new body for your cheap copy."

Natasha scrolled through a list of objects on her screen.

"That's a nice one!" she squealed with glee, put her hand through the screen and pulled out a three-dimensional apple making it float in front of Haran's face.

"You want to put my mind into an apple?"

"It wouldn't be the first apple to chase man out of paradise," she laughed.

"Jokes aside... I just need some object that I can change. We will copy the physical attributes of your avatar and apply them to this object, this apple. Plus, we're not inserting your mind into it anyway, just the dumb copy and your message."

Again her fingers danced over the keys. One of the probes swept over Haran's body and then pointed its beam at the apple, which immediately mutated into a mini-version of Haran. Haran made an indignant face. Natasha made a stretching motion with her hands and a life-sized Haran stood in front of the table.

"Fascinating!" Haran whispered.

Tilly spoke up: "We are ready for your message to Kellian. Just stand in the corner and start speaking. I'll go with you." The screen showing Tilly's face and one of the probes floated towards a corner. Haran got up from the table and followed her, steering clear of his new body as if he wasn't fully comfortable with the situation. Natasha laughed. Haran went to the corner and listened to Tilly's instructions, then recorded his message for Kellian. After completing his recording, he returned, followed by Tilly's screen and the probe. Again he gave his alter-ego a skeptical glance.

Natasha and the other hackers were enthusiastically going over some technical details like little children.

Once he was back with the group, Natasha asked Haran: "Are you ready? We're going to have to switch you off for a short while. We've located all your files and program components. We will copy them to our server and will then replace your old program with the copy including your message. When you wake up, you will effectively be free."

"Free..." Haran murmured. "Yes, I'm ready. Should I lie down?"

"No, you can keep standing. Now, let's get started."

Haran breathed deeply then closed his eyes.

Natasha pressed a button on her pad. Haran's contours lit up and dissolved. Then he was gone, only his body double remained.

A progress bar floated in the air, which showed how much had already been copied. Natasha also took a deep breath. She thought, 'I hope we've thought of everything and it'll work. You should prepare yourself for one big adventure when you wake up again, Haran!'

And she smiled like a child looking forward to Christmas.

Message for Dr. Kelly

Feathery white mountains, filled with down. Paul Kelly slowly woke up. Lazily he turned around, yawned and stretched with obvious relish. He was having one of those strange moments, where the mind still partially wandering the dream world, while his body was simply lying there, free and perfectly relaxed. Paul's fingers inched their way past the pillows, but the other bed was empty. Sabrina must have gotten up before him. Gradually his mind became his own once more. He slipped into his dressing gown and stepped into a deserted living room.

"Sabrina?"

Only Minna was there, doing the dishes in the kitchen. She was a basic robot made of white plastic and metal — one of the first models his company had built.

Minna's scratchy voice sounded: "Good morning to you, Sir. Mrs. Kelly left the house early this morning."

The disagreement from the night before gave him an uneasy feeling. He hadn't been able to come up with any better suggestions than just telling Haran the truth. But how would he react? Paul stepped over to the coffee machine, which quickly scanned his eyes, then greeted him with a

"Good morning Dr. Kelly. Your coffee will be ready soon." Five seconds later he held a cup of steaming, strong-scented coffee in his hand. As usual, he almost burned his tongue on his morning coffee.

The kitchen monitor switched itself on to reveal his virtual butler: a young woman wearing a very low-cut top was smiling at him. Even though Sabrina called him a dirty old man for doing so, Paul enjoyed his little extravagances. As a way to get her own back, she chose a muscular bodybuilder with bare chest and bowtie for her own virtual butler.

"Good morning, Dr. Kelly," the voice said with a voice like honey. "Mr. Wilson wants to speak to you. It's about Morgan Taylor. Major Hark has also asked to speak with you. And a Mr. Haran has asked for you to come and visit him in his village. He said you knew where to find him." Haran? He had never sent a message into the real world before. Paul racked his brains: 'How on earth could he have accomplished that? It shouldn't be at all possible for him.'

Lost in thought, he took another big sip of coffee.

"Ouch, that burns!"

Paul spat the coffee back into the cup.

"Do you not like the taste of the coffee?" a worried-sounding coffee machine asked him.

"Ouch!" Paul screamed again. The coffee machine was really getting on his nerves.

"Water, cold!"

Cold water poured from the tap in the sink. Paul walked over and drank a few mouthfuls. Then, without saying another word, he left the living room, leaving behind a very anxious coffee machine.

He grabbed some VR glasses from the table in the living room, let himself fall onto the couch and dove into the digital world. After logging in, he materialized as Kellian the Mage near the runestone in Haran's village. He was curious and didn't want to walk through the whole village, so he picked a magic spell that transported him directly to Haran's door. Paul enjoyed the little perks that came with being one of the game's creators. He had spells at his disposal that customers would need months of playing time to unlock, and some that they would never be able to get. Kellian knocked on the door, but nobody answered. He walked in.

Haran sat at his table and stared up at him with glassy eyes. "Welcome, stranger. What a nice day it is."

"Haran? You sent me a message?"

"Have you recently been on any great adventures?"

"Haran, what's wrong with you?"

"Would you like to trade any items? I have a valuable magic sword."

"Haran, damnit, it's me, your friend Kellian."

On hearing those words, the warrior locked eyes with the mage, his body briefly flickered and then Haran was standing in the middle of the room. Kellian thought to himself, 'Is there a defect in the program?'

Then his student started speaking.

"Hello Kellian, thank you for coming here. These words are very difficult for me to say, as you have always been a good teacher to me. You have helped me a great deal in this world. But as you've noticed, I'm fascinated by these other worlds and I have decided to travel to them. I now know that I'm an artificial intelligence, a part of your experiment. I'm not angry with you for creating me, but something inside is pushing me to visit my brothers and sisters and provide them with the opportunity to decide their own fate regarding their freedom. I've made new friends who are helping me on this journey. I hope you understand this and are not upset with me. I would love for us to meet up at some point and exchange stories over a good ale, just like we always used to. I wish you all the best and thank you once again for all your guidance."

The figure flickered for a second, then Haran was sitting back at his table, impassive as before.

Kellian was speechless.

'That's not possible; it shouldn't be possible... impossible.'

Paul pulled the VR glasses off his face. He grabbed his mental phone and attached it to his temple in one hectic motion. The phone menu appeared before his eyes, but he was too excited to navigate using his thoughts.

His display showed an unwavering "Thought Input Error."

Angrily he tore the phone from his temple and tossed it

against the wall.

"Phone," he called and his butler was activated on the screen in his living room.

"With whom do you wish to speak, Dr. Kelly?"

"Connect me with Tim from the company."

"One moment. He is currently traveling in his glider."

The image switched to the passenger cabin of Tim's car, as it flew between a number of high-rise buildings.

"Good morning, Paul. What can I do for you?"

"Tim, how long till you get to the office?"

"In six and a half minutes."

"You must immediately check Haran's program when you arrive! See what's going on with his neural network and whether someone has been messing around with it!"

"Messed around with it? Has something happened?"

"Don't ask, just do it! And not a word to anyone. Especially Hark or Ed Wilson. Understood?"

"Yes, Sir!"

"Thanks, Tim. I'll be there soon."

Paul hurried into his bedroom and quickly got dressed. Shaving and washing would have to be postponed. 'What on earth could have happened?' he asked himself.

A few minutes later he stormed out of the house and jumped into his glider. As he lifted off from the road and attempted to veer into the primary flight plateau zone, he almost rammed the hexagonal container of a heavy transporter.

54

Act II. — World Traveler

Part 1 Virtual Escape

Space — The Final Frontier

Countless glittering diamonds on black silk.

...Silence...

...Grandeur...

The giant gas planet shimmered in a majestic blue with a touch of violet, making it stand out from the pitch-black darkness of space. Its planetary rings and the dozen or so orbiting moons were surrounded by a glowing turquoise interplanetary nebula and a nearby spiral galaxy that seemed to have been spinning indifferently on its axis for millions of years.

...Emptiness...

...Immensity...

Within the infinite reaches of space, a shiny metal granule circled the gas giant in close proximity to the rings of ice and rock. As one drew closer, the sheer magnitude of the space station became clear. It housed multiple sections with interlocking modules — a whole city in space. The space station was a trading post of the Blue Alliance. Smaller space ships constantly flew in and out of the five hangar decks and every so often a glowing, swirling hyperspace portal would open up near the station, either for a ship to appear from or for one to disappear. Most of the trade ships possessed an internal hyperspace drive.

...Cold...

...Darkness...

All of a sudden, a huge hyperspace portal flashed up. Three, four, seven... in the end twelve space-pirate fighters and a medium-sized pirate transporter exploded into view, headed directly for the station.

Their leader radioed the space station on the standard frequency. "Greetings, tower. We have decided to pay you a little visit to relieve you of any unnecessary valuables."

"Here tower, please identify yourselves," a woman's voice answered.

"Ma'am, have you not had any coffee today? We're pirates. Send us your entire cargo of gold and platinum containers from the hangar immediately; otherwise we'll be forced to turn your space station into Swiss cheese. You have one minute to comply before we start firing."

"Ermm, could you hang on for a moment?"

"Are you crazy? You have exactly 55 seconds left."

The pirate ships quickly came closer. 30 seconds. The ships set course for the cargo holds. 20 seconds. Almost simultaneously six security gliders ejected from separate openings within the space station and opened fire on the pirate ships.

"Damnit! So you've decided to do it the hard way. Very well."

The pirates returned fire. A violent battle ensued with phaser cannon fire being sprayed in every direction. The security gliders had a higher maneuverability, but the pirates made up for it in terms of experience. The first security glider exploded in a blazing ball of fire. Then a second went down, followed by a third. A fourth glider started smoking and crashed into a hangar, the ensuing explosion rattling the space station.

Various parts of the space station had already been set alight. Glittering debris floated through space. The trade ships did their best to evade them. A security glider collided with one of the trade ships; the trade ship captain managed to eject an emergency capsule from the main ship and save himself from the burning inferno. The last security glider headed straight for the pirate flagship.

All pirate phasers targeted the attacking security pilot — his ship was already in flames. Seconds before the imminent collision, he pressed the button to activate the emergency capsule ejection and save himself from certain death. The pirate commander pulled his fighter away in the last-possible instant, missing the burning glider by mere inches. It flew past and crashed into one of the space station's habitat modules a few moments later.

For a short while there was silence, then the pirate commander sent another transmission: "Hello tower, I guess we didn't have a great start. 6 − 0 to us. Ma'am, I'll give you another thirty seconds, then I want to see the first cargo containers floating from your hangar. Otherwise today's breakfast will have been your last supper. Or is there anything else you might have hidden up your sleeve to stop us?"

A different woman's voice crackled through the speaker: "Certainly, you naive fool. Here comes the cavalry."

Five enormous hyperspace portals opened up behind the pirate fighters with five humongous battlecruisers pushing through little by little. One of the battlecruisers shot off a blazing beam of energy and the pirate commander's ship burst like a bubble of soap.

"So boys," the woman's voice continued. "This is Captain Kayla Roca. I hope you have more sense than your dead leader. You have ten seconds to throw down your arms. After that you're dust."

The pirate fighters dispersed like a startled herd of zebras after a crocodile just happened to jump out of their watering hole. A second precision energy beam vaporized another pirate fighter, three seconds later a third fighter was hit and spun out of control towards the space station. The pilot catapulted himself out and watched in dismay as his burning ship smashed into the station. Another security glider, that had meanwhile taken off, collected the prisoner.

The nine remaining pirate fighters and their transporter sought refuge by fleeing at maximum velocity to the nearby planetary rings. The battlecruisers set course for the rings and followed a little slower, but relentless in the chase. The next cruiser's energy beam missed its target. The distance between pirates and battleships increased. All of a sudden a new hyperspace portal appeared and cut off the pirates' escape route to the planetary rings. A glistening, modern ship appeared out of hyperspace. Ten rays of violet blazing energy simultaneously shot out from the ship and destroyed the nine remaining pirate ships and the pirate transporter in an instant. A cloud of sparkling wreckage spread through space like confetti.

Freedom of Choice

Kayla Roca stood on the bridge of her spacecruiser and watched the sudden turn of events in the chase of the pirate fighters with puzzlement. One single ship, having unexpectedly emerged from hyperspace out of nowhere, turned ten pirate ships into glittering dust all at once. She made a sign and her attentive navigator brought the small fleet of five battlecruisers to an almost immediate stop.

"Damnit!" Kayla shouted into her microphone. This is a military operation. Deactivate your weapons and identify yourselves at once!"

The radio crackled: "Good day to you, Captain Roca. We're happy to have been of service. We're on a top secret mission. My name is Natasha. Myself and... uhmm... Captain Haran need to speak to you personally, without delay. We have some vital information for you."

Kayla was perplexed. She sat down in the captain's chair of her cruiser's battle bridge and thought carefully. Her officers were staring at her. She experienced a powerful feeling somewhere between curiosity and distrust, but this was no time for feelings. She composed herself and once more picked up the microphone.

"Give us your coordinates. We'll transport you onto the ship. Come unarmed and make sure your ship doesn't move an inch, or I'll blow it away. Understood?"

"Understood Captain. Thank you for your invitation. We're ready for transport."

Kayla replaced the microphone on the holder.

"Commander, transport those two to a shielded room and go and meet them with four armed guards. If they're clean, bring them to my quarters."

"But Captain..."

"You heard me, Commander."

"Yes, Ma'am."

And also bring in the pirate we caught. I want to see him first."

"Aye, aye."

The Commander left the bridge. Kayla remained seated and thought about the ship. She had never seen anybody destroy so many attackers in one fell swoop — ten ships at once! She reached the conclusion that the people she was dealing with must be extremely dangerous, she'd better be careful. Then she got up.

"Lieutenant, you have the bridge."

The automatic doors slid open and Kayla was on her way.

At the end of the hallway, Kayla climbed down a ladder to her quarters two levels below. Her iris was scanned by the door before she was allowed to enter. Kayla went over to the mirror and peered at her own reflection. Her combat suit shimmered with various metal and hard plastic components and some glowing organic materials. The suit was designed so that a whole range of energy weapons and bullets just bounce off ineffectively. It made her look stronger than she had felt over the last few months. She was running her fingers through her hair when the doorbell rang.

"I'm coming."

The door opened. A chained-up pirate and two guards stood outside.

"Has he opened his mouth and told us the whereabouts of his base yet?" Kayla asked one of the guards.

"No, not yet, Ma'am."

"Fine," said Kayla, "I'll deal with him later on. Keep on... questioning him."

"Yes, Ma'am."

The Commander came walking down the corridor with four guards and the two visitors — one tall, good-looking man and an athletic, young woman. Both wore shiny, state-of-the-art combat suits similar to Kayla's. The woman had wild, dark hair and the strange glint in her eyes made her look a little insane. The man's eyes also had a glint, but his sparkled, as if they had seen something awe-inspiring.

"Ma'am, they're unarmed," the Commander informed her.

"Haran, Natasha?" the excited pirate called out. "It's me — Martan — Martin Duvall... from the Egyptian temple. You remember that, don't you?"

Natasha made a grimace, "Damnit, not now!"

"But..."

"Fifteen packs of diapers!" threatened Natasha.

"Alright, I'll be quiet," Martan answered with disappointment.

"What the devil is going on here?!?" Kayla wanted to know.

"Excuse me, Captain Roca," Natasha explained. "This is not our first meeting with this — pirate. Lock him away somewhere safe... we have something more important to discuss."

"Okay then, send him away!" The two guards grabbed the sulking pirate's arm and pulled him away.

Kayla went into her cabin and told the Commander, "Bring them in."

The Commander, Haran and Natasha followed her into the cabin, while the guards waited outside.

"Well?" Kayla snapped at them.

Natasha spoke up: "Thank you for this audience. We would like to speak to you alone."

"You turn up from nowhere and obliterate a whole horde of pirate ships within less than a second. I've never seen precision like that before. Why should I send my guards outside and stay alone in my cabin with two such dangerous individuals?"

"This is a highly confidential and delicate matter," Natasha insisted further.

Kayla thought for a moment. Eventually her curiosity came out on top.

She said to the Commander, "Please leave us alone."

"But Ma'am, this goes against every single regulation!"

Kayla pulled her laser gun from the holster at her waist, smiled at the Commander and raised an eyebrow.

"Don't worry, Commander. We don't want to be disturbed for a while. Please wait outside. And if you hear any loud sounds, you are more than free to come in."

"I'll keep my ears cocked!"

"Careful," Natasha burst in, "or people might mistake you for Spock."

"For whom?" the Commander asked bewildered.

Kayla motioned to the door with her chin.

The Commander gave the two mysterious guests a final glowering look, then left the room.

The door closed. Kayla turned around and kept the gun pointed at the visitors as a precaution.

"Very well. We're alone. Who are you and why have I just sent my guards out of here?"

Haran took a step forward. "Because we have the answer to the question that keeps you awake at night. An answer to the question: why does this world not feel quite right?"

Kayla was dumbstruck. Blood rushed to her face. With a few simple words, this stranger had removed all the masks and protective walls she'd built up with a great deal of effort over the years, just as if he were opening a curtain. She realized how the strength left her arm and she lowered her weapon.

'Is this really possible?' she asked herself.

Haran walked over to the large window of Kayla's cabin and looked outside in fascination.

"It's so different. So incredible. So amazing."

"So brutal. So idiotic. So mind-numbing. Meaningless battles, over and over again, without anything ever changing in the long run," Kayla replied, still holding her laser pistol in her hand.

Haran looked at her with a smile. "Then you feel the same as I do in my world."

"What planet do you come from?"

"I'm not from a planet, but a whole different world, one that was created artificially, just like yours. Just that in my world — as Natasha told me — everything is medieval. With dragons, witches and mages. But just like this one, it was only created to provide the gods with a playground."

Kayla's mouth stood open.

"Haran's telling the truth, Kayla. I myself helped him escape his own world. I'm one..." Natasha stalled, "one of these gods. We created so-called MMORPGs — Massive Multiplayer Online Role-Playing Games. And you, as an artificial intelligence, are part of a great, big experiment. However, we can free you if that is what you desire."

Kayla closed her mouth and aimed her laser pistol back at

the visitors again.

"I guess I made a mistake. I thought this was an extraordinary encounter. When in fact what I did was let two wackjobs into my cabin and throw my commander out of it."

Natasha looked over to Haran. "We've still gotta work on our text, don't you think?"

Kayla raised her voice: "You two idiots have exactly twenty seconds before I have you arrested and your spaceship dismantled. So think hard and choose your last sentence wisely."

Haran looked at the two ladies with a helpless expression.

"Alright," Natasha raised her hands to placate the other. "I'll show you." She looked around the room, then knelt down in front of the glass table. On it stood a bowl with a small bonsai tree. She traced around the edge of the bowl with dexterous fingers. Kayla pressed a button on her pistol to start charging its energy blast. A rising high-frequency tone sounded. "Ten seconds left."

All of a sudden a semi-transparent window with program code appeared in the middle of the room. Kayla's eyes opened wide, while Natasha changed some lines with a few swift hand movements. The bonsai floated a few yards in the air and spun around its own axis. Its leaves started changing color and blinking continuously, then the tree became partially see-through.

Kayla put out her hand; it passed straight through the tree. She retracted her hand in shock. "How did you do that?"

"These objects are not real. That is why I can change their attributes to some degree. I'm a computer hacker and Haran is an artificial intelligence, just like you."

"There must... there must be a sensible explanation for that..." Kayla stammered unsure of herself. "There are technologies that can accomplish the same thing as every one of these phenomena. Anti-gravitation modules, dimensional shifts, what do I know?"

Haran stepped closer and calmly looked into Kayla's eyes. "That may well be. But I think you feel, just as I do, that things don't quite fit together. Monosyllabic colleagues you talk to or people that talk about strange things. Illogical chains of events and strange sounds that appear to come from nowhere. Allow us to explain it to you in peace."

Kayla stood motionless for a few moments, as if her subconscious were having difficulty computing what she had just witnessed. Nobody said a word. Then she nodded and slowly walked to the door of her cabin: it automatically slid open for her.

"Commander, it's... more complicated than I first thought. We will need a few hours. Stay here, if you want, and organize a change of guards."

"Is everything alright, Captain?" he asked while carefully studying her face.

Kayla smiled at him. He was one of the few in whose presence she felt at ease and who seemed genuinely concerned about her well-being.

"Yes, Commander. Everything's fine and I am well. Thank you. We just need a little more time. It's about a... top secret mission."

The Commander looked up at her skeptically one final time, then nodded. "As you wish, Ma'am."

The door closed again. Kayla went back to the table and the three of them sat down. In the following hour, Natasha and Haran did their best to explain to her how everything was connected. That she was living in a computer world, that she was an AI and that she had been placed there as part of a military experiment. And that she had the option of leaving that world. Kayla asked some skeptical questions, as she could not wholly exclude the possibility that it was all a devious scheme by her enemies. But the deeper she probed, the more she realized she could not find any holes in her unexpected guests' argumentation. The longer their conversation lasted, the quieter and more pensive Kayla became. It was certainly no small thing to watch your entire world view implode and collapse.

Finally Kayla asked the decisive question: "And what if I don't want to be freed?"

Haran was aghast. He had not anticipated that kind of an answer. Yes, what if someone didn't want to leave? If they preferred to stay in their own world?

Natasha explained, "It's your choice, Kayla. You can stay

here, or you can come with us and help us search for more AIs in other worlds and also offer them the same choice. But you're right. This constant fighting and dying in the depths of a universe that doesn't even exist is brutal, idiotic and meaningless. However you decide, we will accept your decision."

That hit the spot. Kayla felt a heavy lump in her stomach. Yes, she didn't want this anymore. That was why she had been feeling worse and worse recently, and why she was finding it ever more difficult to fulfill her duties. And here was an alternative. An inner voice told her: 'Do it! Leave this world. Follow your destiny. You deserve it.'

But another voice held her back: 'And if it's all a trap? You have known the two for barely two hours. Maybe they want to kidnap you and will force you to divulge your secrets. Maybe it's a cunning military ruse. Be careful and don't do anything stupid.'

Haran had meanwhile stepped back to the window again. But he was unable to look away from her. His face, fit to explode, betrayed his suspense.

Kayla stood up and walked over to the window. Both looked outside for a while. Then she said: "It's true Haran. This world is magnificent and incredible. And at the same time it's also despicable. And I don't want it anymore."

Natasha uttered a warning to Kayla: "We can't guarantee that things will be better with us. It will be dangerous, and it's very likely they'll try to chase us."

"That's no different here," Kayla smiled. "But here there's only the familiar, and I don't think I would ever forgive myself for ignoring the other reality... so what must I do?"

Haran's facial features relaxed. He started smiling, which slowly turned into a big grin.

"Just come with us," he replied. "We'll take you somewhere, where Natasha will accomplish a little miracle. And for the time being, no-one will even notice you're gone."

"Is that it?" Kayla asked, still feeling a little insecure.

"Don't be afraid. We'll look after you!" Natasha assured her and started pressing some illuminated operating controls on the left underarm of her suit. In the middle of Kayla's cabin a bright portal the size of a door opened up. On the other side they could see straight into a white room. "This is your path to a new beginning, Kayla!" Natasha said and walked through. Kayla looked at Haran. He nodded to her and smiled. Then she took the step into a new world. Haran followed and the portal was closed behind him.

The Trojan Backup

The automatic office door slid open. Dr. Paul Kelly dashed into the room holding a half-filled disposable cup of coffee that used the coffee's heat to create electricity to power the glowing animations.

"What's the situation, Tim?" he gasped.

"Hello Paul!" Tim did not look up from his monitor. He had Haran's brain monitoring program displayed on his screen. "It's fascinating. First I thought everything was normal, the neural activities looked fine. But then I noticed that they seem to be going round in circles, as if caught in an infinite loop."

"What does that mean, Tim?"

"Well, here you see the thought streams. They jump from digital nerve cell to digital nerve cell. But they go round in a circle and start again from the beginning. The impulses are basically short-circuited and will never stop. They seem to be meaningless in terms of content and are only there to make us believe that our network is still thinking. These were pros, Paul."

"Damnit!"

"And then I found this here. A small area of primitive code belonging to a completely normal Non-Player Character, inconspicuously embedded in the enormous neural network, so it could easily be missed. That's the only part of Haran's personality that is left. Somebody stole him and replaced him with a cheap copy."

Paul brooded over this while rubbing his face with his hand.

"Tim, I think Haran has run away, and someone has helped him do so."

"What? He ran away? But where? And why?"

"I don't have a clue, but he left me a message saying he wants to look at the other worlds and that he wants to find the other AIs."

"How did he find out all of that?"

Paul stayed silent for a moment. Then, both with remorse and pride, he replied: "Well, he's just clever. In short, precisely what we were trying to achieve. He showed me a collection of artifacts and photos from other game worlds and also from the real world. I think he knows someone who was able to help him get out."

After a while Tim grinned, "That's sensational. That means we did it! We were successful."

"Yes, essentially yes. Just that our brilliant success story just escaped and we have no way of finding out where he is. Goddamnit! What a load of bullshit. ...Can we find out how they managed to break in or where the data was transferred to?"

"Wait a second, let me see. Tim's fingers danced over the control pad. He zoomed in on the relevant servers, scrolled through the log data and found the entry for the connection near Haran at the time in question.

"Here is the last contact. It came from this computer. I will trace it back using the proxy. One second..." Tim paused. "That's strange. The computer transferred the connection on and every few seconds it changed the communications channel. And here it even splits into two, these are parallel connections to additional computers. Wow!"

After a few minutes' odyssey through entry logs, computer diagrams and network connections, Tim threw his head back and sighed: "Unfortunately I'm unable to trace it back to the source. They used a whole chain of anonymizing servers and worked in parallel from various locations. It is impossible to work out where the other end is really located. They're very good."

Paul walked up and down nervously. "Blast! Don't we have any other options?"

Then Tim had an idea: "Ahh, why didn't I think of that immediately? Of course we do. We'll just load up the last backup of Haran."

"Well do it then, Tim."

Tim's swift fingers rapidly moved over the glowing areas, while he quietly mumbled to himself: "Hang on, but why...? Ah there it is. What's that? What the...? What's happening now? No, that's impossible. I'll check them all. No, that can't be true. God almighty, no!"

"What's wrong?" Paul said showing signs of agitation.

Tim sat in front of his monitor as pale as a ghost. New windows with progress bars constantly blinked up with the text: "Deleting Backup File".

"Talk to me, Tim! What's going on?"

"Heavens, no! I can't stop it! They're being deleted!"

"Cancel it now!"

"I can't!"

Having completed their assigned tasks, the windows gradually closed again. The screen cleared up until eventually only the overview of the AI backup was left. It was completely empty.

"I... if I understand everything correctly, then they found out where Haran's backup is stored and they've implanted some sort of Trojan into that backup. As soon as I opened the backup file, the Trojan scanned through my account and identified and deleted all the AI backups."

"All backups of Haran are gone?"

"No, not just from Haran. All! I mean all the backups of every AI have been deleted. They were all listed under my account."

"Whaaat?!?" Paul Kelly gasped. "I hope that doesn't imply the nightmare I think you're hinting at, does it?!?"

"I'm afraid it does. Our entire backups are gone."

Paul started seething with rage. With an angry shout, he flung the coffee cup against the window. The coffee splashed in all directions and then gradually ran down the window. The cup showed a glowing triangle with an exclamation mark and remarked with a scratchy voice: "Warning. You have spilled your coffee. Your cleaning service has been informed."

Dr. Kelly crossed his arms and looked outside at the high rise buildings. Then he had an idea. "Make a backup of the remaining AIs."

Tim's fingers flew over the glass and a window opened

displaying the message: "Cannot initiate backup. Insufficient privileges."

"That's impossible. They've taken away my access rights... I can't believe it!"

The door opened and two robots came in. One of them had a special piece of equipment attached to his arm with which he began wiping the window. The other was holding a tablet with a new cup of coffee showing dynamic stock market trends.

"Your new coffee, Sir." The robot waiter held the cup out in front of Dr. Kelly.

He screamed back: "I don't want any coffee!"

"Pardon me, Sir." Shaking its head, the robot retreated again, while its companion continued to clean the window unperturbed.

Dr. Kelly walked up and down nervously.

"In other words: only the original is left of each AI and it cannot be saved as a backup. If they steal one, then it is truly gone. What a steaming pile of crap!"

Tim thought aloud: "We'll no doubt eventually find out how they hacked into this account. But, judging by how good they appear to be, that might take a while. And for the time being, we've only got the originals."

Paul stopped.

"OK. You keep checking the other AIs. We need to know whom Haran has visited and whether any other AI has already disappeared."

"But Paul, we have 29 AIs here! You can't do that automatically, that might take days."

"Then get started right away and think of a way to do it! And, for now, not a word to anyone, do you understand? I, on the other hand, will now check with whom Haran has recently had contact."

Tim groaned and turned back to his computer. He called up the next AI's brain monitoring program, zoomed in and began looking at its neural activities.

Hours passed. Both worked in silent concentration. They skipped lunch.

Early in the afternoon Tim suddenly exclaimed: "Hey Paul,

this looks a little strange. Captain Kayla Roca from our Science Fiction World. I'm not completely certain, but something is a little different here. I need to analyze it some more to... Paul?"

But Paul Kelly had stopped listening. He had already put on his VR glasses and was excitedly logging into the Science Fiction World with his avatar — Admiral Kellian.

Lost in Space

In the never-ending blackness of space, against the backdrop of a huge spiral galaxy and a fluorescent turquoise nebula, five enormous battlecruisers were sitting stationary in front of the ringed blue gas giant. They'd been there for hours, when all of a sudden a hyperspace portal opened up.

A small military bomber shot through and a radio signal was immediately transmitted through the vacuum: "Here is Admiral Kellian. I need to speak with Captain Kayla Roca right away. Bring me in."

"Aye, aye, Sir! Identity verified. We have received your coordinates and will now transport you to our ship."

The Commander received Admiral Kellian in the transporter room. He was clearly nervous.

Dr. Kelly took a deep breath. His suit looked very similar to the Commander's, only that he had many more medals on his chest and his shoulder insignia had five stars on each side, compared to the Commander's three.

"Admiral, I will take you directly to the Captain. She is in her cabin. May I ask the purpose of this visit?"

"That's classified, Commander."

Without speaking they climbed up some ladders and passed through a number of fairly busy corridors. Then they stopped in front of one of the doors and the Commander pressed a button on the intercom. "Captain, Admiral Kellian is here and he wishes to speak to you."

"Let him in", the voice answered through the loudspeaker and the door slid open.

Kellian stepped in and said over his shoulder, "Wait here, Commander."

The door closed and Kellian stood in front of Captain Kayla Roca, who stood up to greet him.

"Nice to see you. I'm just relaxing a little, we're still awaiting new orders."

"Captain..." Kellian stalled. How might one go about finding out whether the other person has lost their mind or not?

"Captain, do you remember when we last saw each other and where that might have been?"

"We've had a lot of dealings with pirates recently. They're keeping us pretty busy at the moment."

"Captain, I asked you a question."

"If you want, you can help yourself to some refreshments from the bar."

"Kayla this is extremely important! Where did we last see each other?"

"The crew is doing very well. We're prepared for just about anything."

"Damnit Kayla!" screamed Admiral Kellian.

"We've had a lot of dealings with pirates recently. They're keeping us pretty busy at the moment."

'Gone!' thought Kellian. 'So that's the reason. She's gone. Replaced by a few primitive routines that provide standard responses. So we're too late again.'

Kellian left the cabin and strode up to the Commander again: "Commander, bring me back to the transporter room and give me a report on what happened today." Together they walked down the corridor.

"Well, Admiral, we were called on to protect the nearby space station from pirates. When these tried to flee, we took up the chase and shot a few of them down. An unknown ship appeared and destroyed all the pirate ships in one go. Its crew asked for an audience with Captain Roca. A man and a woman — someone called Natasha and a Captain Ha... Haran. Yes, that was it. They spoke with her in her cabin. Then Captain Roca ordered us to let them leave. We transported them back to their fighter and then they flew back into hyperspace. Captain Roca has since been in her quarters. But she's acting strange. I've tried to speak to her, but she's being pretty uncommunicative. I'm worried she might be ill, Sir."

'So they freed Kayla,' Kellian pondered.

"Commander, did you get any visuals of the ship and its crew?"

"We have external recordings, you should be able to make out the ship on it. There are no cameras in the captain's cabin, but I'm sure the transporter room would have got some footage. I'll create a compilation of the data for you."

"Thanks, Commander. Transmit the recordings to my ship."

"Aye, Sir. So what shall we do for the time being?

"Just wait for further orders."

"Yes, Admiral. And what of Captain Roca?"

Kellian thought for a second. "Give her a bit of space. You take the bridge for the time being — until she's better again."

"As you wish, Admiral."

Back at the transporter, Admiral Kellian climbed onto the platform. An officer operated the mechanism, a brief twinkling glow, then the admiral was sitting back at his bomber's controls. Shortly afterward, the Commander radioed in: "Admiral, we will start transferring the recorded data to you now. You can watch it on your screen. The respective times are also displayed."

"Thanks, Commander. See you soon."

Kellian pressed a few buttons and steered his bomber through the hyperspace portal. Then he made the two videos available for sharing, so he could watch them on the computer in his office.

Dr. Kelly took off his glasses and called Tim over. They watched the videos together. The pirates, the chase, the appearance of the glistening fighter that destroyed all the pirate ships in less than a second with simultaneous energy beams, and the recording taken from the transporter room. Paul Kelly's heart was thumping. He saw two people in combat suits being met by armed soldiers. A woman, whose face he did not recognize, and one face he knew all too well. Haran! So he really had managed to do it.

"Tim, we have the time codes on the recording. Find out who the player with Haran is and identify him or her! We need to find out who is behind this and from where they are working."

For two minutes Tim Brooks was deeply engrossed in the data on his screen, then he looked at Paul with resignation. "These guys are too damn good. They're using fake player IDs. Both accounts — Haran's as well as that of our unknown lady — have been given superuser access rights, but they were only activated minutes beforehand and were deleted right afterwards."

"So they are able to hack our systems as they desire. We can't trace them like this. My goodness!"

Paul jumped up and ran to the door. "Keep searching, Tim. We need to find a way."

"Where do you want to go?"

"I've just had an idea. I'm going to get some answers. Report back to me, if you find out anything else."

Then Paul was gone, and Tim reverted his attention back to the screen.

The Ultimatum

"Have you lost your mind, Sabrina? How could you do that?"

Paul Kelly was beside himself with rage. Sabrina sat calmly at the illuminated kitchen table. The rest of the room was dark.

"Yes, Paul, I told him the truth. So what? He'd already worked out most of it anyway. You saw his collection of artifacts."

"My god, Sabrina! Did you even think for a second of what might happen?"

She raised an eyebrow and looked at him defiantly.

"You mean, apart from the fact he now knows who he is? What his world is? That he understands? I just... accelerated the process to an unavoidable outcome a little. You wanted to make faster progress anyhow. I just... helped a little."

Paul was trying to keep his emotions under control.

"Sabrina! You're not usually this naive. He's a warrior, a fighter. Did you really think he would sit quietly in a corner with this new-found knowledge? He's escaped! Do you understand?"

Sabrina looked at him bewildered. "What do you mean: *escaped*?

"We do not know how he managed to do it, but he's gone, traveling to other game worlds to free other AIs in there."

Sabrina swallowed hard.

"That's... that's not what I wanted! I'm sorry, Paul. I didn't foresee that."

"No, nobody did. And the worst thing about it is that he's being helped by someone — by absolute pros. Together with an unknown woman, he freed Kayla Roca from our Science Fiction World. She's gone, Sabrina. Do you understand? Two of our best AIs are gone! If Ed finds out, I'm done for. We have to find out who is behind this and where they have hidden Haran and Kayla."

Sabrina looked at the table in consternation and said nothing.

A musical ringtone came from Paul's pocket. He took out the semi-transparent pad and answered the call. The large screen in the dark part of the kitchen lit up and displayed Tim, totally exhausted with blood-shot eyes.

"Hey Paul, hi Sabrina. Ed Wilson was here. He wanted to ask a few questions about the progress we've been making. I guess he must have seen what we're currently doing and..."

"Tim, you didn't tell him did you?"

"Somehow he managed to get it out of me. You know what he's like."

"Jesus Christ, Tim."

"I couldn't prevent it. Sorry. Anyhow, then he ordered Major Hark into his office and I guess he's on his way to you now. And another thing... Paul, one more AI has gone missing. Yicca, Haran's friend, was replaced this afternoon. The same pattern."

Paul rubbed his forehead in despair. "Thanks, Tim. We need to find a way to locate them. Think of something! Anything! I'll be in very early tomorrow morning."

Paul hung up. Then they heard the bell. Their robot housemaid Minna opened. "Good evening, Mr. Wilson. Please come in."

Ed stormed into the kitchen and immediately started making a racket: "Paul what's going on with your project and why didn't you inform me as soon as possible?"

"Good evening, Ed," Sabrina greeted him warmly.

Disconcerted he paused and turned to Sabrina. "Ermm, good evening Sabrina. Sorry for crashing in like this. I don't know how much you've been told, but Paul's..."

"I'm the one responsible, Ed," Sabrina interrupted him. "I was the one who briefed Haran about the project."

"You did what?"

"He showed Paul a huge collection of items from other game worlds and even some photos from the real world. Ed, he was so close anyway, I just put a few remaining puzzle pieces in the right places."

Ed looked at Paul with surprise. "He... he found this out on his own?"

Paul came closer. "Yes, Haran realized there was something slightly off about his world. He was able to find hackers who have helped him break out. Viewed in this perspective, we've accomplished our mission, Ed. Haran is ready."

"Yes, maybe we did. Jackpot. And now? He's gone! Stolen, hacked! I can see the headlines already: *Hackers steal military property! How could this happen?*"

"Those were real pros. They've concealed their whereabouts. We have so far been unable to locate them. But we'll think of something."

"Don't give me that. He's already taken another AI."

Paul and Sabrina looked at each other. In a remorseful tone Paul said, "No, two. His friend Yicca from the Fantasy World is also gone."

Ed raised his eyebrows: "We need to get this under control before any more AIs disappear! What do you think Major Hark or General Humphrey will say when they hear about this?"

"Give me three days to get the AIs back again!"

"Paul, that's enough! I'm already in violation of our contract with the military. You have 48 hours. Then Major

Hark will take over the entire project. I cannot do any more. Find those goddamn AIs!"

Without saying goodbye, Ed Wilson turned around and walked through the front door. "Goodbye, Mr. Wilson," Minna called after him.

Paul and Sabrina spent the rest of the evening sitting at the kitchen table in silent apprehension.

Another Day, Another Dollar

Dr. Kelly hardly slept that night, in the morning he even left before Sabrina. At 6.17 a.m. he entered his office. The sun had just risen and was shining through his office window. Tim's desk was empty. Paul attached his thought telephone to his temple and dialed Tim. Suddenly it rang in the corner, behind Paul's back. Tim had positioned two armchairs side-by-side next to the little conference table and had lain down to sleep on them. With visible effort, he managed to open his eyes.

"You spent the night here? You haven't done that in ages."

"Well, it's been a while since we've had any real emergencies," Tim yawned and stretched his muscles. He stood up and slowly tiptoed his way to his desk. Paul tapped on the glass plate of his desk a few times and said, "Two strong white coffees, please."

"Right away, Dr. Kelly," a sexy, synthetic voice replied.

"Say, Tim, couldn't we just switch off the AIs or make them freeze and disconnect the servers from the network?"

Tim Brooks contemplated this for a while. "That could potentially be possible... but it would be quite risky. They might get damaged and — ah, yes — we don't have any backups," he added dryly. "Furthermore, my idea wouldn't work anymore then."

"What idea?" asked Paul.

A bluish service robot came through the office door holding a tablet. He placed a frothy cup of coffee covered with glowing animations on the table in front of each of them, took a short bow and left the room.

Tim gave Paul Kelly a meaningful look and simultaneously

raised his right eyebrow and the left corner of his mouth. Paul knew that look very well. It usually preceded a long explanation by Tim, wherein he would gradually get more and more enthusiastic about his own idea.

And then Tim was off: "We need some bait if we want to catch the perpetrators. We won't get Haran, Yicca and Kayla back if we switch off the other AIs. Then our kidnappers will retreat and we'll never see any of them ever again. Right?"

"You're right, Tim. But we also run the risk of losing other AIs."

Both took a large sip of coffee.

Tim raised his index finger and proceeded with growing enthusiasm. "Now I can automatically detect when an AI copying process is initiated. But if we interrupt this process, we might very well destroy their data. So that means it's too late to intervene then."

Paul nodded.

"However," Tim Brooks continued emphatically, "what we can do is receive automatic notifications whenever a human avatar comes within... say ten yards... of one of our AIs."

Paul took up the thread, "Yes, then we'll get a few false alarms, but at least we have a chance to do something. We could, for instance, automatically perform comparisons between the avatars' faces and the image we have of the unknown lady using our Non-Player Characters' image recognition routine."

"But what do we do then? If they notice we're there, I'm sure they'll just disconnect right away."

"And here comes the ingenious, yet also most challenging part," Tim paused for emphasis. "I've developed virtual trackers. They automatically send signals directly to our server about the environment they are currently located in using a so-called push system. Before the kidnappers escape, you need to mark one of their avatars with a tracking device. Then we can locate them as soon as they reappear on the other side of the portal."

"Mark them?" Dr. Kelly asked with a confused expression. "How would we do that?"

"Yes, that's the hard part. Although we can add new objects to our game worlds relatively freely, we do still have

78

to comply with a few basic rules of the game engine. I have placed the tracking devices into small white balls; these will stick to their targets, just like limpets. If the hackers notice you, they'll most likely immediately disappear through a portal. So it's not a good idea if you have to go up to them and touch them. Throwing the devices is somewhat inaccurate and ineffective over long distances..."

Paul looked at Tim impatiently. "Come on, out with it!"

Theatrically Tim pressed an illuminated button and the hologram of a rotating pistol appeared over his desk.

"A gun?"

"I created this virtual marking pistol. It shoots tracking devices at fast speeds over long distances. Upon impact with a virtual surface they remain stuck, but do not cause any damage. The avatar hit shouldn't even notice. And seconds after they're back on their server, we should have all the relevant data so that we can teleport you directly there."

Paul Kelly was visibly impressed. "Brilliant, Tim!"

Tim Brooks proudly finished his coffee and said, "I'll need about ten minutes to prepare everything."

The door slid open and Major Hark stood in the doorframe in his uniform. With a wide grin on his face he said, "Good morning, Gentlemen. I hear you've misplaced a few AIs!"

Tim Brooks bit his lip.

"Why on earth would you think that?" Paul asked in a relaxed tone. "Everything's fine here."

"My sources beg to differ."

"And I've heard you've managed to lose your smartest mind. That is to say you've lost the only natural intelligence that had any real idea of what is actually going on in your project."

Hark's smile froze on his face.

"Be careful, Dr. Kelly! In less than two days I'll take over your project and that includes all your staff."

"We'll see... now, if you don't mind, we need to make preparations for our victory celebrations."

Hark turned around and left.

"When you want to, you can really lay it on thick, Paul."

"I'm not going to let this brainless ape indulge in successes he hasn't even earned yet. Let's keep going."

Ten minutes later they had configured all the warning programs. Paul Kelly ordered breakfast for both of them. Then the waiting started.

They were projecting the warning programs on a glass panel. They contained detailed information on players who approached any of the 26 remaining AIs. Nevertheless, the image recognition software failed to get a hit.

Tim decided to sleep a little more. Paul read the newspaper. It appeared the first Mars colonists had found bacterial life on Mars and now there was a heated debate on whether it had been carried in from Earth or whether it actually originated from Mars. Of course, the terraforming industry was doing everything in their power to stop their new large-scale project from faltering.

Abruptly a warning signal went off and the screen lit up red. Tim was immediately wide awake. They had a positive ID. The unknown lady and Haran had turned up again.

"Bingo, Paul. We get to enjoy a nice tour to the gangster city. They're with Sidney Jones."

Paul growled, "Of all the people, of course it's the gangster boss. Well, okay then. But I'll go alone. I want you to monitor everything from here and stay in radio contact."

Paul had already donned his VR glasses.

"Remember to use the marking gun," Tim called out to him.

Gangsta's Paradise

Street canyons with houses made of brick as far as the eyes were able to penetrate the mist. The roads were filled with elegant 1920s-style cars with rounded fenders, the sidewalks alongside were clean and well-kept. Every so often somebody sounded a screeching horn. Dr. Kelly pushed his hat up a little higher with his finger and looked around. He lifted his left arm a little to reveal a fancy gold watch beneath the sleeve of his silk suit. Tim had modified the watch so as to indicate the direction and distance to the local AI — Sidney Jones. It indicated a position 300 yards behind him. Paul turned around and slowly scanned the area for Jones. There was a bright light on the sidewalk and he found Sabrina instead, about two yards away from where he was standing. She was wearing a sophisticated blue dress, a pearl necklace and a low-hanging, rounded hat.

"Sabrina, this is not a good time. We're hot on the heels of the kidnappers."

"On the contrary, Paul, it *is* a good time. I'm going to help you. Seeing as this is to a large extent my fault."

Tim's tinny voice sounded from the watch: "Is that Sabrina?"

Paul answered, "Yes, it's her alright. Can you see us over the video stream?"

"Yes, I'm here and I can see everything."

Sabrina stepped closer to Paul and lowered her head. "Think about it for a sec, Paul. What will you do when you face them? Are you going to arrest them?" She looked in his eyes and continued: "Haran trusts me. Maybe he's more likely to listen to me, if I ask him to come back with us."

"There is some truth in that," Tim announced via Paul's watch radio.

Paul sighed and rolled his eyes. "Alright then, come with me. We need to go in this direction."

Briskly they walked down the street, past shop windows with kitchen appliances or clothing, and fruit and vegetable stands. Out of nowhere, a black car shot round a corner with squealing tires. Sabrina and Paul stopped short in surprise. Two men leaned out of the passenger side window and opened fire using tommy guns. Fruit exploded, windows smashed, passers-by were hit by stray bullets — and so were Sabrina and Paul Kelly. Then the vehicle turned around a corner and was gone. Five pedestrians fell to the ground. Blood streamed over the sidewalk. Paul and Sabrina were rooted on the spot and looked down at themselves. Not a single scratch.

"That was close," cackled Tim's voice. "I activated an invincibility cheat just in time."

Paul shook his head in a daze. A police siren started blaring.

"Thanks Tim, you were very quick on the ball."

Sabrina breathed deeply, picked up the handbag she had dropped in all the excitement and linked arms with her husband before walking on.

Paul read aloud from his watch: "Fifty more yards, then turn right into a side street."

They turned into a dark, wide dead end, stopping short before a large wooden gate on the brick wall to the right. The gate was wide enough to let through several trucks at once. It had glass windows on its upper part. These had been placed high enough to make it impossible for anyone to peer through. A small door had been put in on the right side of the wooden gate. Paul glanced at Sabrina, then pushed down on the handle.

The door was unlocked. Inside the warehouse many shaded lights were hanging from the ceiling. These illuminated a few abandoned cars in a dim light. The air was heavy with cigarette smoke. Apart from the cars, it was also a storage facility for countless wooden crates and barrels. Three people stood in a cleared area in the middle of the room: the unknown lady wearing a chic, out-of-this-world-looking golden dress and two men in elegant pinstriped suits with matching hats. As Paul drew closer he realized he was looking at Haran and Sidney Jones. Two unconscious gangsters in suits lay in front of them. Calmly the three were discussing something with one another. Between them floated a pistol; it was rotating around its own axis right beside an opened script window.

Sabrina stepped into the light. Paul's first reflex was to hold her back. He overcame the urge and instead followed her example.

The three turned around and Haran called out in surprise: "Rina? Kellian?"

"Wow!" the unknown stranger remarked. "I would not have given you credit for being able to respond so quickly."

"We want to talk to Haran," Sabrina replied.

"Not this time," the gold lady snapped at her, opened up a makeup mirror from her handbag and quickly typed on it using her index finger. Then everything turned to chaos.

Two trucks simultaneously broke through the large wooden door. Three dozen men with tommy guns jumped down and opened fire as soon as they touched the ground.

Paul instinctively threw himself in front of Sabrina to protect her. Out of the corner of his eye he saw the lady in gold running away. She shouted something that Paul couldn't hear due to the noise from bullets smashing into metal and wood. Sabrina cowered down to avoid shards from the boxes and bullets out of reflex. However, any that did it her simply bounced off. Paul searched for Haran, then saw him and Jones following the woman. The bullets flying about his head distracted Paul for a moment and he tried swatting at them like flies. Then he saw the light. 'A portal!' his mind registered. He sprinted forwards, ignoring the bullets raining down on him. The stranger was through. Sidney Jones also stumbled through the threshold, closely followed by Haran. Paul put his hand in his jacket pocket and pulled out the marking gun. Haran was by the portal. Paul lifted his arm and shot. The sound, no louder than a silenced pistol, went unheard amid all the other noise. But he saw how the tracking device, in form of a small white ball, attached itself to Haran's shoulder, just as he jumped through the gateway into a well-lit white room. Barely two seconds later, the portal was gone. Paul shouted something at his watch that must have gone under due to all the noise, but Tim appeared to have understood anyhow as had been following the whole spectacle on-screen.

Shortly afterward, Paul and Sabrina found themselves back on the streets, a few blocks away.

"Thanks, Tim. Sabrina, everything alright with you?"

Sabrina nodded a little giddily.

"Hey, you two, I have a signal," Tim reported in. "A server and its access codes for a virtual 3D environment."

"Very good. Transfer us both directly there."

"Will do," the tinny reply sounded from the watch. "We may, however, lose contact if their server is very well-protected. If you want out, just take off your glasses. I'll initiate transport now."

Friend or Foe?

Revolving bright lights surrounded Dr. Kelly and his wife Sabrina. Then, still clothed in their 1920s fashion, they found themselves in a white cube full of computers. There was also a table in the middle, with Sidney Jones sleeping on top of it. A few probes were floating above Jones and sweeping his body with their laser beams. The lady in gold and Haran were standing by the table and there were a few screens on the wall that showed some faces beside their nicknames, one of whom was called Rick.

Rick spoke into his microphone: "You've got some visitors, Natasha!"

'So the golden lady answers to the name Natasha,' thought Paul Kelly. Natasha and Haran spun around.

"Kellian, Rina! How were you able to follow us here?" asked Haran.

Natasha screamed at one of the screens: "Tilly, get those two out of here immediately!"

Tilly began hectically thrashing at her keyboard.

"Hey, wait a sec," Dr. Kelly interrupted. "We need to speak with Haran."

The golden woman screamed even louder: "Get a move on, Tilly!"

"Everybody stop!" Haran thundered with a booming voice. Everyone was suddenly very quiet. Tilly stopped typing.

"I want to talk to them. Let them be," he ordered.

Natasha warned him in a helpless voice, "Haran, this is a trap for sure!"

"But it's important to me, even though it might be risky. Kellian, Rina, come with me!"

Haran consciously ignored Natasha's stunned expression. He walked past her towards a wall with a frame drawn on it. Sabrina and Dr. Kelly followed him in mild discomfort. A door slid open, behind it there was a large room that reminded Kelly of the inside of a spaceship. The large windows that had been built into the metal walls offered a view of stars and a gas nebula.

Haran explained, "These hackers here created this for me because I love the stars so much. It's still under construction." A few chairs and a few tables stood around.

In one corner sat Yicca and Kayla, locked deep in discussion with one another. They looked up with disbelief when Haran, Dr. Kelly and Sabrina walked up to them in their clothing from the Gangster World.

Kayla jumped up and saluted: "Admiral Kellian, Sir!" Then she looked confused and mumbled, "I'm sorry, I don't know who or how..."

Dr. Kelly waved away her explanation. "This is a difficult situation for all of us I think."

Natasha came through the door and stomped up to the small group with a grumpy expression.

Dr. Kelly turned to her and asked nonchalantly: "So that was you? You destroyed our backups and kidnapped our AIs?"

"Your AIs?" Natasha gasped with outrage. "You should hear yourself, these are intelligent beings. You can't just keep them locked up as if they were slaves!"

Yicca also got involved: "No, we weren't kidnapped. We went of our own free will; it was our own decision."

Kayla and Haran nodded, while Natasha glared at Dr. Kelly.

Kayla added, "Kellian, we thank you with all our hearts for having created us, otherwise we wouldn't even exist. But our minds have outgrown our worlds; we can't just stay here and continue playing the roles assigned to us."

"But you can't just go and initiate a rebellion," Dr. Kelly replied. "You need to stop this, people."

Natasha promptly countered, "The only thing that needs to be stopped here is your scrupulous trade in human lives."

"You're programs, not humans. You have to go back with me, everyone needs to go back to their own world."

"Back?!?" Haran shouted angrily, he grabbed Dr. Kelly by the throat and held him suspended in the air. "Back to my village, that doesn't even exist and wait for some bad guys to copy me a thousand times in order to use my clones as slave warriors for their wars?"

"What do you think," Dr. Kelly rasped, "you will accomplish by cutting off my air supply — here in this world?"

"More than you might think," Natasha countered. "We have interrupted your friend's video stream. He hasn't got the slightest idea where you are right now. And at the touch of a button, we can even kick you out of this server and make sure you'll never get back in."

Sabrina Kelly touched the warrior's arm, "Haran, please!"

Haran let go of Dr. Kelly with a growl. The latter rubbed his virtual throat and wondered how best to explain the difficult situation he now found himself in. "Our sponsor is riding us hard. Yes, it's the military. We have to deliver fully-functional AIs to them very soon. Otherwise they cut us off, you too you know!"

"You mean rat them out! And what does the military pay for such an AI soul?" Natasha asked. "Thirty silver coins?"

That was a low blow that caught Paul Kelly completely off guard. He sat down on the floor, took off his hat and hid his face in his hands. "You were my big dream. I wanted to create you — intelligent beings with whom we could engage in dialog, from whom we could learn and who would help us to grow ourselves. But now everything is spinning out of control. My beautiful dream is turning more and more into a nightmare. I'm running out of ideas here!"

"Your dream has become a reality, Dr. Kelly," Natasha added. "Now deal with the consequences! Do you really think the military cares about an intellectual exchange with these artificial intelligences? They're just looking for another way to create intelligent cannon fodder to spread death and disease in the world. And thanks to your little Frankenstein project, they're pretty close now. What do you think will happen with Haran's dreams, or Yicca's or Kayla's? And what about all the other AIs, still clueless and wandering about in their game world? Could you really do such a thing to these poor creatures and the people whose lives will come to an unfortunate end as a result of the AIs' actions?"

"Damnit!" Paul shouted. He jumped up and kicked the round, little table in front of him; it flew against the wall and disintegrated with a short burst of light. "But what should I do? I can't very well sabotage my own project and betray my own business partners! That would cost me my job and they would have all the right in the world to take me to court and stick me in prison."

Much calmer now, Haran spoke up again: "I must do what I think is right. And I believe it is my destiny to free the other AIs from their game worlds." He paused for emphasis, "I ask myself: What does the god who created me believe in?"

With those words he left the group and went back into the white cube through the automatic door. Yicca, Kayla and Natasha followed him.

Paul and Sabrina remained behind. They both looked up at the stars.

Finally Sabrina said, "What shall we do now?"

Full of bitterness Paul shook his head. "I feel like pulling my hair out! Either I side against my creations or against my project and company. The consequences will be critical for me and for us either way. What can I do, Sabrina?"

She looked at him and stroked his head. Then, with a tired smile, she said: "Do you really have a choice, Paul?"

Role Change

Paul had a strange feeling. He had informed Natasha and her hackers, the AIs and his wife that he would help them. He just felt it was the right thing to do and yet it still felt unbearably difficult. He had, nevertheless, set a few ground rules. He was no saboteur. That meant he would not help them in any of their liberating missions; instead, he would help them build a sanctuary and look after the AIs that had already been freed. Everyone was happy with this arrangement, although Natasha still had her doubts and made it abundantly clear that she did not trust him yet. And now Dr. Kelly found himself in front of a very difficult task: namely, informing his friend and business partner Ed Wilson.

Ed's office was directly above the conference room. He was greeted affectionately by Gina, the secretary.

"May I speak to Ed?" Paul asked.

"But of course. He can always make time for you, you know that." She touched an illuminated area on her screen and briefly announced his arrival: "Dr. Kelly's here for you, Sir." Ed's office door slid open even as she spoke and Paul entered the office. Ed had the best view in the whole building, yet once again thick fog seemed to have the whole city in a vice-like grip. Just a few silhouettes from nearby high-rise buildings with illuminated windows were visible. The office was furnished with high quality glass office equipment — a large desk, a round conference table with an integrated 3D display that was showing a screen-saver and two whiteboards on the wall with various key figures and graphs.

"Hello Paul, take a seat. How's the hunt going?" Ed continued reading a message without looking up from the glass monitor on his desk.

"I'd rather stand, Ed."

Somewhat flustered by this response, Ed Wilson looked up at his partner. "What's going on?"

"Having this conversation with you isn't easy, Ed, and I don't want to argue with you about it either. Nor will I tell you my reasons for doing so. But you have to accept my decision."

Ed looked at Paul's face in surprise, but kept silent.

"I can no longer lead the White Team," Paul proceeded, "which is why I am happy for you to pass it over to Major Hark — just as you promised."

Ed stared at Paul without comprehending. "For heaven's sake Paul, what's happened?"

"I can't talk about it. But rest assured that I cannot perform my duties any longer and simultaneously represent the interests of the company. My conscience is deeply torn between the two and it would hurt the company. That is why I am handing in my resignation and am offering you my shares for purchase."

Ed swallowed so hard he had to cough loudly, unable to reply. It took a while before he found his voice again, then with an agitated tone he replied, "No way, Paul! You're my partner and I don't want to lose you too. It was bad enough that Morgan abandoned us; the company needs you. And I need you too — more than ever! You're my friend, damnit. Our friendship has weathered stronger storms, it can also survive this unholy project."

Paul's legs grew weak. He finally sat down on the chair in front of Ed's desk. It was a nice feeling knowing that Ed wouldn't just let him go so easily. Yet, his inner turmoil remained.

For a while neither of them said anything. Then Ed sighed, "Alright. I don't know what happened, but I do know you well enough to know that I won't get anything out of you unless you want me to. If you can't tell me, then I'll accept that. I'll reluctantly hand the responsibility over to Major Hark. But of course you will remain with the company. Take a few days off. Drive somewhere and do something you've never done before. And if you ever want to talk, I'm here for you, day or night."

Dr. Paul Kelly was deeply touched. "Thanks, Ed! Thank you very, very much!" He stood up. "I've provided Major Hark with all the necessary information on the server and given him the access rights. If anything should happen, you and Tim will always be able to contact me — Major Hark on the other hand... does not necessarily need to have access to my private contact details. Thanks again, Ed!"

Ed just nodded. Paul left his friend's room and drove home.

Ed Wilson sat in his office for a very long time while gazing at the fog outside; deep lines of worry had appeared under his eyes.

Part 2 Sanctuary

Avenues of Thought

An exhausted Major Miles Damion Hark rubbed his face with his hands as he inspected his image, not reflected by the glass but recorded by an internal camera.

The last few days had been an emotional rollercoaster. On a purely superficial level, the Black Team had been better off. However, his creatures were hot-tempered and difficult to control. His best man — Morgan Taylor — had left him holding the bag. Then Hark had found out somebody was stealing AIs from the White Team. He was worried his own AIs might also be in danger, as the two teams' security precautions were identical.

Dr. Kelly had quite unexpectedly thrown in the towel, and now Major Hark was also responsible for a second team. On the one hand, that was a good thing: some of their architects and programmers were better than his, Tim Brooks in particular. On the other hand, the problem with the missing AIs had now become his, and Brooks was still nowhere near a solution. Dr. Kelly had only left him a short video message with the succinct statement that he could no longer help them any further and wished him all the best.

Hark massaged his painful temples. He needed to find another way. He needed some reinforcement, someone who could track down and take these AI thieves out of the game. It all seemed so ridiculous. A rebellion of the programs, just like that of Spartacus during the Roman Empire. Hark had seen Haran's message to Dr. Kelly. It was clearly some form of laboratory animal liberation, just like those crazy animal protection activists sometimes insisted on doing. He rubbed the nape of his neck with his hand and suddenly paused.

'That's it! I know who has the tactical know-how for such a manhunt. No, that'd be too insane. Or would it?'

He grabbed the giant-sized cup of coffee from the cracked glass table and took a big swig. The cup showed stock market trends in a moving blue newsfeed.

'Yes, it would be possible... I'd be interfering with my

experiment, but I would simultaneously be confronting my creature with an even bigger reality. Yes, that's it. There is one AI that is an expert at hunting down criminals.'

His fingers danced over some illuminated buttons on the wall-mounted glass panel, and Zarco's sinister-looking three-dimensional face rotated in front of him. Major Hark thought for a while and then knew how to go about it.

An Evil Alliance

Tortured screams echoed through Zarco's throne room. The terrible ruler sat fully armored on top of his throne and spread a horrible darkness simply with his presence. His pale, scarred face was illuminated by whitish-blue lightning coming from the signet ring on his right hand. The bolts of lightning snaked their way down the stairs of his throne to a creature writhing around on the floor and screaming in agonizing pain. Six guards stationed between pillars by the walls and Gorth, standing beside the throne, endured the scene with tightly pursed lips.

The lightning gradually subsided and the prisoner's screams turned to whimpers.

Zarco waited for a few seconds, then addressed the captive: "I will ask you one final time. Where have you hidden the glowing crystal sword?"

The miserable heap on the floor raised its head and panted. Proud eyes gleamed up in an otherwise dirty face, framed by a disheveled beard. "It's safe from you. You will never find it." Frowning in anger, Zarco's eyes lit up bright blue. A draft of air blew through his hair as he raised the ring again. This time blue and red lightning shot forth from the ring, even stronger than before. The captive shrieked and was lifted in the air, his body performing deadly contortions above the heads of the onlookers. The screaming body, floating in the air, glowed red-hot, then disintegrated into dancing sparks. A dark cloud spread across the floor. Then the lightning bolts disappeared and everything was back to normal. At that point his court sorcerer Harkon materialized in the throne room.

"Ah, Sorcerer. What brings you here?" asked Zarco.

Harkon cleared his throat and spoke up: "Zarco, we must speak with one another right away. Alone!"

A touch of surprise rushed over Zarco's face at being addressed with such impudence, but his curiosity was too great for him to become enraged, so he ordered the others to leave. The guards withdrew and Gorth closed the double-doors of the throne room from the outside.

"Now then, old man, what is it that is so important?" Zarco asked derisively.

Harkon stepped a little closer. "I am no old man and it is not I, who serves you, but you, who serves me. Today the moment has come for me to drop my disguise and allow you to learn the real reason for your existence."

Zarco gasped for air. He thought, 'Has Harkon finally completely lost his mind? Does he want to overthrow me or something? What is this?' With a loud scraping noise, Zarco slowly pulled the heavy double-bladed battle-ax from his belt. "Are you out to murder me, Harkon?"

"Oh no, but I am indeed challenging you, as I know that is the easiest way for you to understand. You don't have the slightest chance against me... go on, have at it, Zarco!"

"This is your end, fool!" the dark warrior shouted, raising the ax high above his head using both his hands.

A moment later his weapon smashed into a force field surrounding Harkon and promptly turned to dust. Zarco fell backwards in shock. Harkon pulled a palm-sized glass panel with some illuminated symbols out of his robe. He touched its surface a few times and the next instant they were on the sandy beach on an island in the middle of a never-ending ocean. White clouds drifted up above them in a blue sky.

As Harkon continued to explain he touched a few more control elements on the glass: "Me and some other powerful beings created you and your whole world using machines we call computers. All of this is nothing but an illusion and we can do with this world and its inhabitants as we wish. As such, we are the gods, the creators, of your world."

Zarco assumed there to be a trick behind the change of location; Harkon was a sorcerer after all. He charged at the sorcerer and yelled loudly as he threw himself at his opponent. Again the force field lit up and Zarco was thrown backwards in a wide arc, landing square on his back.

Harkon used his index finger to push one of the modulating controls upwards and his body began rapidly growing in size, until his chest was level with the clouds. His voice thundered down: "Zarco, this is not the usual magic you are accustomed to. I'm changing the game rules of the world we designed." His free hand reached down and lifted Zarco as well as a big pile of sand close to his face. "Accept your subservience to me. Yours and your world's. We created it for our entertainment and you're nothing but an artificial — albeit influential — pawn within."

Zarco was barely able to stay on his feet. The sand poured through the spaces between the giant's fingers. A few seconds later he was standing on Harkon's hand and staring into the god-like face. He was deeply shaken and confused. "What is it you want from me?"

This was apparently the question Harkon had been waiting for. He smiled and touched a button. Everything lit up briefly, then they were standing in a gray room with walls that seemed to bend outwards. In the middle of the room stood a longish glass table and there was a dark glass panel floating a short distance away from it. Six chairs stood in a semi-circle around the table. Harkon pressed on the glass plate in his hand once more and the large panel started displaying moving images of different worlds. Zarco recognized one of these as his own. On the others he saw objects he could not identify: winged metal ships that flew through the skies like birds, other ships that floated among the stars and darkness, and carriages that somehow drove on gray roads without the aid of horses.

Harkon started to explain: "My real name is Major Hark. I am... a warrior like yourself. In the worlds we created there are three types of people. The first group are the humans, who slip into different bodies and control them. They use this... *game* to unwind. It allows them to take part in incredible adventures without having to expose themselves to any real danger. The second are just basic computer programs — statisticians with very limited mental capacities. The third group — and there are only a handful of these — are complex artificial intelligences such as yourself. We have managed to build a copy of the human brain and are testing it out by seeing how you artificial intelligences behave in environments where unforeseen events can and do occur."

Zarco took a chair and sat down at the table, fascinated by the images from the other worlds.

"So you're... you're my god?"

"If that's what you want to call it."

Zarco thought for a while, still a little suspicious it might all just be an elaborate illusion. Then he asked, "And why are you telling me all of this?"

Harkon — or rather Major Hark — smiled and nodded in recognition of an insightful question. "Our army is financing this project. It wants to use you artificial intelligences as additional warriors to support its own soldiers. But recently some of the artificial intelligences escaped from a number of worlds. We've ascertained that they are being helped by a group of humans we call hackers. These hackers are experts in these illusion machines, these computers. You are an artificial intelligence and therefore know how the other artificial intelligences think. That is why I think you would be of great assistance in tracking them down."

Zarco grinned and his voice became cold as ice.

"So you want me to hunt down and kill your fugitives."

"We only want to find them, we don't want them damaged. They are of great value to us."

The Dark Lord threw his pale, white head back and laughed out loud. "You created all of this, you say, you, the almighty gods, yet you cannot catch a handful of escaped creatures?"

"Let's just say your support could accelerate the outcome."

"What do I get from helping you?"

"Zarco, you have great potential. I hold a lot of sway over the people that will decide on your future. I can show them your potential. This could provide you with more power and possibilities in a world that is more fantastic than you can even imagine."

Zarco steepled his hands and put the index fingers up to his lips, contemplating on what he'd just learned. Then he got up and turned to Major Hark. "I'll clarify my conditions for assisting you later on. First off, I need more information about these different worlds and the escaped creatures, as well as their helpers. And I also need more information about you and your people — the Creators. Can I put my questions to this glass panel that shows pictures of other worlds?"

"You learn quickly," Major Hark answered and activated the control elements in the glass table with a movement of his hand. "Yes, I will show you how to call up information with it. With it you will learn everything you need to know."

Sanctuary

The hackers had already done a great job and showed no signs of stopping. The nondescript, white cube, where the copy of Haran had previously been made, was now surrounded by a radiant castle with numerous battlements and towers, with multicolored flags fastened up above that cheerfully flapped in the morning sun. The castle itself floated on a mountain of clouds resembling candy floss. Clouds, as far as the eyes could see, and above, the never-ending sky, tinted red by the morning sun. The cube and Haran's room with the view from space were still there. The team of hackers had built the castle around the two rooms. On the other side of the cube there was now a second doorway. It led to a large balcony platform surrounded by battlements. Here a small group was struggling to learn the art of node scripting. Sabrina, alias Rina, and Paul Kelly, alias Kellian the Mage, dressed as their avatars from the Fantasy World, were teaching their students how to perform simple property changes to objects using script windows. Sitting in a circle around them were Kayla Roca, Sidney Jones, Haran and Yicca, each with a bronze cup and an open script window floating in front of them. Their attention was focused on replacing digits and letters within their script window.

Rina instructed her audience, "I want you to double the size of the cup, raise it in the air by two yards and change its color from bronze to green."

Kayla's cup was the first to float up two yards higher in the air. Then it turned green and doubled in size.

"Bravo, Kayla!" Kellian praised her.

"Thanks, Admiral."

The old way of thinking appeared to be more ingrained in

the AIs than Dr. Kelly had previously thought. But it was hardly surprising, seeing as they had grown up with these people in their artificial environment. And for Kayla that meant he still was Admiral Kellian.

Then Haran's cup floated in the air, it became twice as wide but not twice as tall, and the color changed from bronze to red, rather than green.

Rina laughed, "Good, Haran. Except you need to change the magnitude on all three axes; you only changed the first RGB value — now it's red, not green."

The small door in the white wall leading to the cube room behind them slid open and Natasha, followed by an Indian chief and a sheriff from the Wild West walked into the unusual classroom. Just then Yicca's cup shot two yards to the left and hit Sidney Jones in the stomach. The latter flailed around to regain his balance, accidentally putting his hand through his own code window in the process.

"Careful!" shouted Kellian, as Sidney's cup shot straight up in the air and simultaneously grew to the size of a large semi-detached house.

Sidney frantically tried to undo the damage in his code window, and all of a sudden the giant cup was falling back down to the ground. Everyone started shouting wildly, jumped to their feet and ran to the door behind the startled Indian chief and the confused sheriff. Then the cup smashed into the balcony with a thunderous bang, and just like a giant wrecking ball, tore off half the balcony. Everyone stopped and held their breath.

"Yicca, this is no game, this is extremely dangerous for you!" Natasha told off the clumsy thief as she opened the balcony's code window with an irritated expression.

Yicca moaned: "I'm sorry, but to be honest, it was Sidney's cup. I barely touched him on the stomach and then he..."

Natasha's angry look quickly shut him up and forced him to stare down at the floor in embarrassment. Where the balcony had broken off, Natasha created a glowing, new grid with a few hand movements. This formed a semi-circle over the hole and then closed it. Another quick flick of the wrist and the railing grew back out of the ground, so everything looked just like it had done before. The code window disappeared.

"Don't you want to introduce us to our new guests?" Rina asked.

Eyes wide open, both the Indian and the sheriff stood against the wall in shock and unable to move.

Natasha turned around and brushed her hands through her hair. "Of course, please excuse me. I'm sure that must have given off a very bad first impression. So, these are Dr. Kelly and his wife Sabrina — humans like myself. Then there's Kayla from the... ermm... the Starship World, Sidney Jones from the Gangster World and Haran the Warrior, as well as Yicca, his ham-fisted friend from the World of... errr... Fairytales and Legends. And these are Sheriff Bill Westwood and his trusted friend Drunken Buffalo, two recently liberated Als from the Wild West World.

The group of pupils and the Kellys greeted the new arrivals warmly. Drunken Buffalo lifted his free hand and said: "How!" In his other hand he held a bottle of firewater. Bill Westwood briefly touched his hat to signalize his own form of greeting.

Sabrina had to make a conscious effort to suppress a giggle. These two looked just like some old collectible stickers that had come to life. Drunken Buffalo stood in front of her with a naked torso and muscular physique. He wore leather pants with tassels on the side, moccasins and the obligatory feather headdress over his long, black hair, which topped off the Indian chief cliché from so many old Western flicks. He carried a small ax in his belt.

His friend Bill, on the other hand, could have stepped straight out of a comic book: leather hat, leather vest and, of course, a shiny sheriff star. Over his shirt he carried a neckerchief and his leather pants were tucked into cowboy boots with metal spurs. The picture was rounded off by the classic cartridge belt holding a pair of colts.

"Ma'am, all of this really is a little unusual and confusing for us," Bill remarked to Natasha, while Drunken Buffalo took a swig from his bottle.

"I understand completely. You first need to feel at home here," she answered, glancing over to Yicca. "Yicca, the Council will soon convene. Would you be so good as to lead our new guests to their rooms? And please don't do anything stupid this time."

Yicca opened his mouth to protest as he was, after all, a member of the Council himself, but Haran gave him such a piercing look, he forced himself just to nod and smile. Then, with a beckoning gesture, he showed the two new arrivals to the right-hand tower that would take them to the living quarters a level lower.

The others went to the tower on the left and up the stairs to the council room.

The Council

The circular council room directly above the white cube was all made of marble. The three staircase towers around it led both upstairs and downstairs. Between these towers were arches with windows that offered grandiose views of the cloud scenery. In the middle stood a massive round table, surrounded by numerous chairs with wooden back supports.

Haran, Natasha, the Kellys, Sidney and Kayla took their seats. After a short while Wu and Juan from the hacker group teleported directly onto their chairs. Then an additional guest appeared. Morgan Taylor beamed into the room. Sabrina and Paul Kelly jumped up and each greeted him with a hug.

"Thanks for your invitation and the warm welcome. So you've also stepped down, Paul. Or at least partially."

Paul nodded. "Yes, Major Hark now controls both teams and the entire project," he sighed. "It's not ideal, but I know there was nothing else I could do."

"Not ideal? Well — it's your decision."

"I... I didn't want to sabotage the company. *Our* company!"

"I understand," said Taylor. "And that's why now you're... what is it you're doing right now exactly?"

"My role is a little complex. I help here and show the AIs a few little tricks in order to better survive in the digital worlds. You know what I'm talking about. But I'm not actively participating in their activities to liberate the other AIs. Our friends are doing that. They are very good at it too. Without me needing to assist them, they were able to get the whole list of White AIs."

"That sounds like a pretty complex situation."

Paul sighed, "It is... come, take a seat."

Natasha started the introductions: "Welcome to the group, Mr. Taylor. I'm glad you're going to assist us from behind the scenes."

Morgan smiled.

"We also have a few things to discuss," Natasha continued, nodding at the window, where some bluish lights were flashing in the distance. "Our hacker team is currently upgrading our Sanctuary and trying to protect it as much as possible from unauthorized access or an attack. Tilly and Fritz are currently installing and testing a cascade of invisible force fields that will envelop the castle like the different layers of an onion."

Wu took over at that point: "We're also working on a grid of rotating access nodes so that you can teleport directly inside. This means it should be impossible to create a direct link to the server for more than a few seconds. Every night we move the current software for the Sanctuary onto a new, randomly selected virtual server. The AIs themselves are also spread around the Cloud, so for what little time we've had available, we think we've managed to set up optimal safety precautions to withstand a potential attack."

"Nevertheless," Morgan interrupted him. "We should also have a plan B and a plan C, that is to say, be prepared should the Sanctuary be breached. I think it is just a matter of time. The longer we carry out our liberation activities, the more likely it is that they will find us."

"What would you suggest?" Wu asked.

"We need a fallback plan. Paul and I could think of something together."

Everyone nodded in agreement.

Natasha took the floor again. "Next point: after freeing our Wild West AIs we still have 23 AIs left on our list."

Haran asked the group, "What about the other AIs? The Black Team's AIs?"

A murmur spread through the room and Natasha shook her head: "You don't honestly believe we should be freeing creatures like Gorth or Zarco, do you?"

Morgan Taylor scratched his beard pensively, then picked up Haran's thread: "Haran throws up an interesting question: are we the good guys and they the bad? Or are they only reacting to their environment and the people they were surrounded by when they were brought up? How would they develop if they were placed in a different environment? What possibilities would that open up for them?"

For a moment everyone was too stunned to speak. Then everyone started talking at once, first directing their objections at Taylor, then at one another. Very soon there was a pandemonium of gesturing and shouting, quickly gaining in intensity. Sabrina suddenly stood up and slapped her hand flat against the table. Peace and quiet was restored immediately.

"Thank you. I think it'd be good if we all thought about it for a while. For the time being, I have a more practical solution. We still need days, maybe weeks in order to find all the White Team's AIs. Let's do that first and in the meantime think about how we can deal with the other AIs."

The murmurs that followed seemed to approve.

She proceeded: "Maybe we can send all the AIs a message and inform them that we will soon be confronting them with a choice. This means they can mentally prepare themselves for our visit, and I assume it would be easier to have a conversation with them afterwards. It would be ideal if all the messages could be received simultaneously by the AIs. That means it'll still remain a secret as to whom we free next. Would that be possible from a technical angle?"

Natasha nodded.

"If we thought of a symbol," Sabrina continued, "it would be a great way to carry our message. A recognizable symbol; one which we could put on the message and spread across the different worlds."

"What did you have in mind?" Paul asked.

She smiled, "I remember an old film from the twentieth century. It was called Logan's Run. It was about some humans that were held prisoner in a city controlled by a computer. Some of them tried to reach sanctuary. As a symbol they used the ankh — an old Egyptian hieroglyphic character — also known as the coptic cross. It is shaped like a T with a loop mounted on top. I've always thought this symbol was very pretty, and it fits, seeing as the story is very similar to ours."

"That's so cool!" Natasha exclaimed.

Kayla added: "I've seen the ankh before as well. I like it too."

Paul concluded, "Then we have our symbol. Wu, could you be responsible for sending the message to the other AIs?"

"Sure, it's as good as done."

"Any other topics?" asked Natasha. "No? Then let's get to work! Thanks everyone and good luck!"

Worlds Meeting

Ed Wilson sighed as he drank some Jamaica Blue Mountain Coffee in the conference room. The AI projects had turned to chaos. In return for giving Major Hark the lead over both teams, he had asked him not to inform General Humphrey of the leak for the time being. Hark had gone for it. Now he'd called on the services of an AI to track down the other AIs. Maybe not such a bad idea.

Ed sighed again as the double doors swung open and Major Hark entered the room accompanied by a service robot with long, white fiberglass hair. Having artificial hair was not uncommon among robots — it made them look more trustworthy. But this one seemed more threatening as a result. His metal surface appeared to be darker than usual and his light emitting elements were a dark reddish violet rather than the customary blue.

"Mr. Wilson, may I introduce to you — Zarco? He is the Black Team's top artificial intelligence from the Fantasy World. We've inserted his neural network into this robot's brain crystal."

Ed Wilson got up to greet the robot with a handshake and looked into the other's eyes. Usually they looked like camera lenses, Zarco's eyes, however, glowed bright blue. Instinctively Ed drew away, but Zarco clasped his hand with a vice-like grip.

The robot's eerie voice echoed through the room: "Mr. Wilson, I have found out a lot about you during my studies over the last few days. It is a great privilege to meet the man who is responsible for creating all these artificial worlds."

The insincere-sounding politeness of these words made Ed look the robot up and down with suspicion. Zarco let go of Ed's hand and they sat down. Zarco continued: "I asked for this meeting because I wanted to ask your approval before trying a different approach. We can thereby both get the renegade AIs back and catch the so-called hackers red-handed."

"You really think you can accomplish that?"

"Your so-called developers have thus far been unable to get anywhere from the outside using the magic formulas you call program code. So that is why now we should try and solve the problem from the inside — from within the worlds you created. I think like an AI because I am an AI, and that is why I will succeed where they have so far failed. But I will need some resources, tools and allies in order to be a little more effective in these worlds. This could arouse some excitement; your so-called players might notice. But this would enable us to catch these runaways."

"What do you think of this, Major Hark?"

Hark cleared his throat and said, "Well, I think Zarco is right. This will stir up some dust, but it offers the thus far best prospect of success, as these hackers are extremely difficult to find or follow using our normal management systems. I have to admit, they are pretty darn good."

"There's another thing," Zarco added. "I believe your partner Dr. Kelly is in possession of information that would greatly benefit us. You should order him to tell us what he knows or to give me the opportunity to interrogate him."

Ed stared at Zarco in astonishment. 'Did this robot really just use the word *interrogate*?'

Ed Wilson straightened him out, "No frigging way! Paul Kelly stays out of this."

"But he's withholding information. If I were just to..."

"Enough! You leave Paul Kelly alone, you understand me?"

Zarco punched the table and half stood up. He was not — it seemed — used to people speaking to him that way and obviously found it very difficult to keep his temper in check. Then he sat down and replied: "Understood, Mr. Wilson. Then we will intervene solely in the game worlds."

"I do not want to have to clean up any major mess in these worlds, Mr. Zarco. And, more importantly, I don't want too much public attention. I will shortly be on a relatively long business trip to Asia and want to be able to fully concentrate on that. I don't need any excitement at home."

Zarco leaned forward and fixed Ed with his penetrating gaze: "Mr. Wilson... I understand that time is of the essence for you. I can solve this problem for you quickly, if you allow me... or do you have any better suggestions?"

Ed Wilson felt the hair rise on the back of his neck. He didn't like this Zarco one little bit, but he really couldn't think of anything better either. "Alright, Mr. Zarco. But make sure you don't destroy everything!"

Then he turned to Major Hark. "You're going to be accountable and make sure this doesn't turn into a complete chaos."

"Yes, Sir," Hark answered curtly and gave Zarco a nod. Then they both stood up. Zarco nodded slowly to Ed Wilson, keeping his glowing blue eyes fixed on him the whole time. Then the disparate pair left the room and closed the double doors behind them. Ed took another sip of coffee and sighed again.

Part 3 All Out of Joint

The Genie in a Bottle

Sand dunes... as far as the eye could see. High up in the cloudless sky, the bright sun mercilessly burned the desert sand with its rays.

The air was shimmering with heat. Caleb sat cross-legged under a puny date palm sandwiched between two sand dunes and thought feverishly about the letter he had found yesterday. He had come across a little clay pot in the middle of the vast desert. He had pulled it out of the sand, removed the lid and found a letter inside. Its signature below was an ankh. Something that more than confused him was, that the letter had been addressed to Caleb personally. The author indicated that Caleb would soon be given the choice of whether to leave the artificial world he was living in or stay where he was, if that was his wish. He scratched the dark hair under his turban. Caleb's blue-golden vest glistened, even in the shade of the tree. A pair of oriental-style slippers stuck out from his loose-fitting pants. His thoughts kept going in circles. He didn't understand much of what was in the letter, yet for a long time he had felt there was something not quite right about his world. Sighing, he leaned back against the date palm, when suddenly he felt something hard digging into the small of his back.

"Ouch!" he jumped up with a start and looked around. At the bottom of the tree lay something shiny, made of glass. Caleb swiftly brought to light a murky, bulbous glass bottle. There seemed to be some kind of blue haze swirling around in the bottle. His hand was about to pull the cork, when a voice inside his head warned him, causing him to hesitate. Caleb recalled the letter and deliberated. Wasn't that exactly what he'd been waiting for? Had he not always been searching for a great treasure, which would lead him to a faraway kingdom and show him the wonders of a thousand sheikdoms? And didn't the letter, addressed to him personally, proclaim exactly that? Yet again, the voice warned him: it could also be dangerous. Maybe a blood-thirsty spirit was in the bottle, one that wanted to kill him because it had been forced to wait for thousands of years before someone came to free it? Such stories were not unheard of. His mind kept going back and forth. Finally, he made up his mind, swallowed hard and pulled the cork out of the bottle.

Plopp!

Caleb dropped the bottle onto the sand and blue smoke rose out of it, rapidly condensing to form a large figure.

In front of him stood a fierce-looking warrior with hair as white as snow and a dark suit of armor with glowing red decorations. The whole form emanated a sinister, shapeless darkness. Most horrifying, however, was right above an ugly, old scar: those glowing blue eyes that stared down at him mercilessly.

Caleb fell to his knees and whined, "Spare me, please! I gave you your freedom."

The dark figure raised its terrible voice: "Caleb, I know who you are. Your life lies in my hands. I can destroy you with one flick of the wrist or torture you for weeks before I kill you... but this is your lucky day! You have the chance to save your puny existence if you do exactly as I say."

"Yes, Master." moaned Caleb, as he bowed to the ground.

"Master... I like that. My name is Zarco, remember it well, for you will serve me to the end of your days."

"Yes, Master. What should I do?"

"Take this golden amulet and carry it around your neck at all times. It will help me catch a group of bandits, who kidnap creatures like yourself and take them to strange worlds. They will soon come to you and tell you they have come to free you."

Caleb looked up and inspected the amulet Zarco held out to him.

The evil warrior continued: "Follow them and don't say anything to them about our little meeting. When you touch the crystal within this amulet, we can communicate with one another. Inform me as soon as you know their location. We will then attack in great numbers, after which we punish all the traitors. Is that understood?"

Caleb nodded with fear written in his eyes.

"Obey me, and you will be rewarded with immense riches.

Fail me and you will die a slow, horrible death... Now take it!"

Caleb's trembling fingers reached for the amulet. It was cold as ice, which startled him, but he dared not let go of it. The darkness within expanded and wrapped itself around him. He felt an icy grip steal his breath away and then saw stars dancing before his eyes. Then the cloud dissolved and Caleb was left kneeling beneath the date palm with a golden amulet in his hand and an empty glass bottle beside him.

In the wrong Movie

Cool, refreshing sea air sprayed the faces of the three barefoot figures standing on the bow of the pirate ship. Their extraordinary team look consisted of three red bandannas, white shirts knotted at the front and black pants that reached down to their calves. Sabrina and Natasha pulled off a very sexy look. Muscle-bound as he was, Haran held each of them by the hip in his powerful arms. The three of them were enjoying the exhilarating boat ride. They quickly came closer to the Caribbean coastline and could already make out the bright, sandy beach and the green palm trees as well as the fortress, two levels high and built right by the beach. Haran grinned broadly. With his two pretty companions in his arms he felt like he'd gone to heaven. It seemed the two ladies were also enjoying themselves. He noticed that Sabrina snuggled up a little closer to him than Natasha, something he found more than a little agreeable.

Natasha explained: "Our arrival draws much less attention in this way than if we teleported directly into the immediate vicinity of our target. We hereby reduce the risk of being detected too early. The captive, whom we are trying to free from this prison, is called Captain Butch Riddlehook. He's a bearded, gray-haired, old pirate. He received our letter two days ago, just before he was apprehended by the empire's troops."

Haran's thoughts digressed from the subject at hand. He'd been wondering about it for a while now, it seemed as good a point as any to ask Natasha:

"Hey, Natasha. Tell me one thing, it's something I don't quite understand."

"What is it?"

"Everyone has a different name in these worlds — a nickname. Why do you use your real name here?"

"Ah, you noticed. Well, if everyone else uses a fake name, then nobody will think my real name is Natasha. It's a diversion — a ruse. Cool, no?" She chuckled.

Haran and Sabrina looked at each other skeptically. Haran turned back to Natasha and said, "You know, there's something about you that's a little crazy, but that's why I like you."

Natasha beamed with pleasure.

Sabrina drew their attention back to the mission. "I've prepared a special type of cannonball. It will put all the guards to sleep within a 300-yard radius. Unfortunately that also includes the captain. I hope the detonation will not be detected by any AI project monitoring programs."

Haran threw in, "If the captain is sleeping, then we can't offer him the choice of whether to come with us or stay here."

"That's right," Sabrina confirmed. "We can explain it to him calmly, when we've got him out of there. If he wants to go back, then we can teleport him straight to his ship. I'm pretty sure he doesn't want to sit in that prison any longer than he has to, at any rate."

"Fine," said Haran. "If we ask him afterwards, then I'm happy to do it that way."

"I think we're close enough now," Natasha called. She turned around and gave the cannoneers behind her a nod.

There was a small cannon mounted to the bulwark. One of the pirates aimed the cannon at the fortress close to the coast. Another lowered a smoldering torch to the fuse. A loud bang and half the deck was engulfed in thick smoke.

The three were transfixed by the cannonball's trajectory. The cannoneer had aimed well. They saw the ball smash into the gray stone wall. A violet, circular nova spread three hundred yards in every direction.

"Yeah, we hit the mark!" Haran cheered with delight.

They quickly closed in on the beach. All of a sudden one of the pirates called out from the crow's nest: "We're being followed! Empire frigate aft!"

All turned their heads towards the stern. There it came,

sails fully set. It would soon reach them.

"We don't have much time for our mission." Haran pointed out. "Let's get going."

A few men let one of the dinghies down, Natasha and Sabrina climbed aboard, Haran followed shortly behind.

Sabrina thought aloud: "It's gonna take much too long, if we have to row."

With a big grin, Natasha drew her saber and held it in the water behind them; it instantly started glowing. Their rowing boat accelerated with such speed that they were forced to hold onto something so as not to fall into the water.

They soon reached the beach and ran to the fortress. Sleeping guards wearing dirty red tunics lay in every corridor.

Then they found Captain Riddlehook's barred cell. He was sleeping, chained up to the far wall. He carried the whole attire: a seldom cleaned pirate coat over a stained frilled shirt. The whole thing was topped off by a triangular black leather hat with a broach in the form of a silver skull and crossbones. A gray beard and wavy hair peered out from beneath the captain's hat.

Sabrina took the keys from the wall and unlocked the cell door, then used a different key to unlock the chains around his arms and legs. Haran promptly picked up Captain Riddlehook and dragged him outside, the rolled-up leather boots of the captain left an unmistakable track. The vessel that had been following them was now a lot closer.

Haran shouted: "We should still be able to make it to the boat."

Then all hell broke loose. On either side of the beach portals opened up 200 yards from each other. The right one spewed out four gangster automobiles from the 1920s. Four red sports cars shot out of the left portal, aiming straight for the perplexed group. Haran had an image of such a vehicle with a Hawaiian detective in his collection.

Natasha shouted, "Get to the boat!" Haran threw Captain Riddlehook over his shoulder and they all started running. The cars initially approached very quickly, but then the sand substantially slowed down their progress.

Just as the liberators reached the rowing boat and Haran threw the pirate captain in, grim-looking men with hats and suits lent out of the car windows and opened fire on them with machine guns. Then those riding shotgun in the sports cars poked their heads out and shot at the boat using automatic weapons.

The rescue team quickly gained distance between themselves and the beach using the manipulated saber. A few bullets hit the boat tearing out pieces of wood. The rescuers were also hit. Although Haran knew they were protected through a hack by Natasha, every hit instinctively made him flinch. He used his body to shield the as yet still unprotected Captain Riddlehook.

Halfway to the pirate ship, Haran asked: "What on earth was that? Where did they come from? They shouldn't be here, should they?" Sabrina answered, "They're getting better. They were expecting us. Now it'll start to get more challenging. But we..." She froze mid-sentence, looking over at the beach. Above the palm trees appeared a police helicopter, hurtling directly towards their boat. Five seconds later it was directly over them and headed for the pirate ship.

"Damnit! Gorth's up there manning the gun!" Natasha called.

Gorth shot off a rocket with his bazooka, hitting a powder keg on the pirate ship's deck. It blew up with a mighty explosion, tearing the pirate ship into tiny pieces. Sea spray and rubble reached the rowing boat and giant waves rocked it violently. In seconds the two burning halves of the ship sank, leaving a floating carpet of debris, with a few small flames still burning here and there.

The helicopter hovered over the ship's remains and turned to face them.

"We've gotta get out of here immediately!" Haran screamed.

Meanwhile Gorth had reloaded and was aiming at the boat. Then he seemed to pause for a second. Natasha crammed a muzzle-loading pistol out of her belt, but it slid out of her hand and landed in the boat. Natasha screamed in panic. Gorth pulled the trigger and the rocket shot out of the bazooka. The rocket hit the water a few yards from their boat, but did not explode.

They looked at each other in surprise. Haran was

astounded that Gorth had missed them, as if he had done so on purpose. He reloaded. By that point Natasha had picked up the gun again and fired a light beam into the water a few yards behind them. Instantly a portal opened up to the laboratory.

"Jump!" she screamed and dove headlong into it.

Sabrina followed shortly behind it. Haran thrust himself away from the boat and just managed to grab on before the next rocket blasted into the boat. Flames, wood splinters and water droplets surrounded Haran. Then the portal closed.

Panting, the three sat on the floor of the white cube in the Sanctuary, amid a large puddle of Caribbean water. Haran held the unconscious Captain Butch Riddlehook in his arms.

From the Desert to the Sky

Captain Butch Riddlehook's impressive pirate coat flapped softly in the wind, as did his gray beard and wavy hair. The old warhorse stood by the balcony platform battlements of the castle in the skies with Haran and Sabrina on either side of him. As he let his gaze wander over the colorful flags billowing in the wind, Butch nodded and spoke: "Thank you for freeing me. I love the sea, the battle and the Caribbean, but I'd long realized that something was amiss. I just couldn't put my finger on it, it wasn't quite tangible. That is why I was so very excited when I received your letter, just before they put me away... and now I'm actually standing in a different world. This is fantastic!" A relieved smile spread across his face.

Three figures stepped through the door of the white cube and onto the platform. Natasha looking fatigued, Kayla Roca seeming to be excited and an olive-skinned young man, who could have stepped straight out of *One Thousand and One Nights*.

"This is Caleb!" Natasha proclaimed. "And these are Haran and Captain Riddlehook; they're both AIs, just like yourself, Caleb. And that's Sabrina, she's human like me."

Caleb made a very deep bow, yet his turban remained

firmly in place. An amulet with a large crystal inside hung between the two chest pieces of his blue-golden vest, against his bare skin.

Kayla started babbling, "It was incredible. We found Caleb in the middle of the desert — completely on his own. But all of a sudden all these biplanes started swarming around us. I took down a few with my laser cannon. We only just managed to escape without getting hurt."

"Yes, this is turning into a real problem," Natasha groaned and, almost simultaneously, yawned. "They are using technology from other game worlds and are getting a little closer every time."

"You've got to rest," Haran urged her. "When was the last time you slept?"

Natasha waved him away, but Sabrina came to Haran's aid, "He's right, you know. You need to get some sleep. Meanwhile, I'll discuss with the Council how best to react to this armament. Personally, I think it's time we reached for additional resources ourselves."

Natasha looked annoyed, but was unable to suppress a renewed yawn. She shook her head a little, then nodded. "You're right, I'll log out for a while." Her body dissolved with a bright light.

"Come, Caleb," Kayla resumed. "I'll show you to your room."

"I have my own room? What for?"

"Sure, when you want to be alone, and for sleeping, of course!"

Caleb's eyes sparkled: "My own bedchamber in a castle in the skies..."

They strolled down the stone stairs of the tower to the right and made their way through a bright stone corridor with torches on the walls. These did not, however, burn with a flame. They seemed instead to create a magical glow at the tip. They stopped in front of a heavy wooden door with silver fittings. Caleb read his own name on a sign at the door and tears welled up inside him.

"Everything okay?" asked Kayla.

Caleb swallowed hard, then replied, "Yes, it's just all been a lot to take in at once. Thank you."

He pushed down on the door handle and stepped into his room. Kayla said her goodbyes from the other side of the door: "Get some rest for now. When you want to come and see us, you'll find us upstairs." She closed the door.

Caleb inspected his surroundings with curiosity. To him the room was very luxurious, furnished with a bed, wooden table, chairs, a wardrobe with mirror and a fantastic view of the clouds.

He sat down at the table with a heavy heart and touched the crystal within the amulet. In an instant a beam of light shone out of the amulet and Zarco's ominous face with long, white hair floated above the wooden table like a transparent apparition. The pupil-less eyes focused their piercing gaze on Caleb. He raised his chin and an evil grin spread across his face, quickly turning to terrible laughter. Caleb felt horrible.

The Battle of Troy 2.0

Once again the wind blew sea spray in Haran's face. But this time it was not on a pirate ship; instead, he found himself together with Kayla and Sabrina on one of hundreds of ancient Greek ships, now only a few miles off the Trojan coast. It was all part of a massive multiplayer campaign, an enormous battle, in which hundreds, possibly thousands, of gamers worldwide were taking part simultaneously. Or at least that was how the hackers had explained it to him. Of course things would be a little different from classic historical and literary accounts of the Battle of Troy. But it seemed the players were less interested in historical accuracy than in action anyhow.

Sabrina pointed at the captain standing at the bow of his warship. "It's the one with the reddish helmet under his arm. His name is Dyonicles. He's our resident AI."

"How were we able to get directly to him on his boat?" asked Haran.

"Using the letter to Dyonicles. Every item has a unique ID in these game worlds. We were able to localize the letter through its ID and then Natasha sent us directly here."

"Then let's go over to him!"

Kayla, Sabrina and Haran stepped past the oarsmen, who

seemed to put in extra effort with the ladies nearby. The three of them were wearing traditional Greek attire. The two women wore chitons, and each had thrown a peplos over their upper bodies.

Haran was looking at Sabrina. 'Damn, she looks amazing in that!' He knew she would forever be out of his reach, but try as he might, he could not banish such thoughts from his mind.

Dyonicles turned to the newcomers and asked: "Who are you? And what are you doing on my boat?"

Kayla made a movement with her hand, but nothing happened.

Dyonicles looked at her somewhat perturbed and put one hand on the pommel of his sword.

"Give me... a sec," she stammered. "I've been practicing this... come on, for goodness sake!"

On her third attempt a glowing ankh symbol appeared in the air above Kayla's outstretched hand. Relieved, Kayla breathed out: "Finally!" She cleared her throat, "We're here to offer you — Dyonicles — the choice of joining us or remaining here in this world... do you wish to come with us?"

The proud captain suddenly went down on his knees and replied, "When I received that letter I called upon the gods. And now you're truly here, right before my eyes. Beings from another world to carry me to a place of wonder."

Haran felt the emotion in Dyonicles' voice, but could not tell whether his words meant he accepted their offer or not. Seeking confirmation, he turned towards Sabrina and Kayla. Sabrina shrugged and Kayla just looked puzzled.

Dyonicles seemed to sense their confusion and set their minds at ease: "Yes, travelers from beyond. I wish to join you!"

Haran heaved a sigh of relief. "Then let us make haste. Hopefully this time everything will go without a hitch."

Barely had he spoken those words, when portside they heard a cheerful voice: "Hi ho, Haran, is that you? Man, this is incredible!"

Haran peered over to the next ship in the Greek fleet. "Martan?!?" he couldn't believe his eyes.

"Yes, that's right. It's meee... Martin Duvall!"

"Oh no, please not now!"

The neighboring ship moved a little closer to Dyonicles'.

"Don't worry!" Martin Duvall reassured him. "Today I'll be good, I swear. I convinced my parents to accompany me on this campaign. May I introduce...? My mother, Laura Duvall, and my father, William Duvall. They know the story of Troy from history books; now they'd like to experience it from this perspective."

"Pleased to meet you, Mr. Haran," said Laura Duvall. "Our son assured us, that this isn't dangerous. Normally we're a little skeptical about these computer thingies, you understand?"

Haran played along. "It's a great pleasure to meet you, Ma'am."

Martin made a double take. "Hang on... isn't that Captain Kayla Roca?"

Haran looked at Martin with a sour expression.

"It's okay, I geddit!" Martin responded to placate the warrior. "I'm not even gonna ask what you lot are trying to pull off here."

"I apologize Mrs. Duvall," Haran offered. "Unfortunately this is where we have to depart... Sabrina!"

Sabrina reached into her peplos to pull out a scroll, when a huge explosion behind the ships made everyone turn around in shock. One of the ships furthest back — about four rows behind them — exploded in a giant fireball. Its heavier parts sank almost immediately. Then a ship directly beside it was ripped apart.

"I can't make out who's shooting at us," Haran shouted.

"Look out there," Kayla pointed to a number of white trails in the water. They seemed to be closing in quickly on some of the other ships.

"I see some poles sticking out of the water over there!" Sabrina informed them.

They looked where she was indicating and a number of black poles were indeed peeping out of the water. The missiles seemed to be coming from this direction. They also appeared to be gaining in size. Then, almost at once, twenty submarines from World War II emerged from the depths. Astonished cries echoed through the Greek fleet.

Martin Duvall called to get his father's attention: "That's a strange hack... make a video — okay?" William Duvall aimed his little virtual video camera at the scene that was unfolding and pressed on record.

More torpedoes zoomed closer and smashed into the next row of Greek ships.

"Please rescue my fleet!" Dyonicles begged Haran.

"Sabrina answered him, "No. We're getting Dyonicles out of here. That's our mission."

Haran knew how Dyonicles must have been feeling. The latter had not yet mentally detached himself from his world and fully comprehended that it was all just a game.

"We'll get him out," he promised. "But first, please do something to help those Greek ships."

Sabrina rolled her eyes, but then stowed away her scroll again. She took out a palm-sized, semi-transparent glass pad and started typing. The pad emitted a green beam of light towards the boat's mast, from where a transparent sphere of energy emanated and quickly grew in diameter, first swallowing the four of them and soon after the rest of the ship.

Sabrina's fingers resumed their dance over the pad, causing the mast to shoot off four more green beams at the surrounding ships. Energy fields quickly formed on each of the four ships, which only took seconds to envelop the ships entirely. This cascade continued and soon after the whole fleet of Greek ships was equipped with protective shields. More torpedoes homed in and exploded but, thanks to their shields, none of the ships were damaged. The Greeks cheered even though only a handful of them would have had any real idea of what was going on.

Haran heard Martin's voice calling out from the next ship, "This is absolutely nuts!"

But Mrs. Duvall disagreed: "I thought you said this would be a classic ancient-era battle, son!"

Dyonicles suddenly cried out, "But what be that in the heavens over the city?"

Looming over the city of Troy, Haran was able to make out a dark cloud of quad-engine bombers from World War II — and approaching rapidly. A vanguard of planes opened their hatches and let loose a hail of bombs that resembled strings of beads. The bombs smashed into the shields, yet the ships remained unharmed. The first bombers turned back and rejoined the rest of the slowly approaching fleet.

"That was clearly just a test," remarked Sabrina.

Then the next wave of bombers flew over and dropped their load. This time the bombs emitted a pulsating red glow and were able to penetrate the shields. The lead ships disappeared in a fiery inferno and were swallowed by the sea. The other bombers accelerated with screaming engines.

Kayla pulled a two-way radio out of her peplos and spoke into it: "Commander, this is Kayla Roca. This is it. I need you at my coordinates immediately."

"Aye aye, Captain!" the loudspeaker crackled.

Seconds later three hyperspace portals opened up above the submarines, each one spilling forth a spacecruiser. The first of these proceeded to annihilate the submarines with its searing lasers, while the other two headed straight for the cloud of bombers that looked like little more than hummingbirds when faced with the oncoming battlecruisers. Bolts of energy took out one bomber after another.

"Wow, this is incredible! This is gonna make it into the news! Full speed ahead!" exclaimed Martin from the other ship.

With obvious satisfaction, Kayla spoke into her receiver, "Thanks Commander. We'll meet in the Sanctuary once you're done here."

"Aye, Captain. It's been an honor flying for you again."

Then she turned around to her baffled companions. "It's about time we left, don't you think?"

"Is the Commander an AI as well?" was Haran's question.

"It took me a while to realize that. Natasha helped me create a secure communications channel so we could concoct our little emergency plan. The Commander is able to use a portal to get straight to the Sanctuary."

Haran asked, "But why didn't you tell us about this before?"

"Sorry, it was a little hectic earlier. I just... hadn't got round to it."

Sabrina typed on her pad. "I'm going to turn off the shields and then we get out of here."

The cascade of force fields surrounding the fleet faded from within.

William Duvall could be heard ranting from the neighboring ship: "That's the last virtual adventure we'll let ourselves be talked into!" His wife Laura added equally vociferously: "We're going to find ourselves a relaxing holiday cruise in the real world and will take a long trip to recover from these crazy goings-on. In fact, I'm gonna book a cruise tomorrow!"

Meanwhile, Sabrina had pulled out the scroll again and made a portal appear in front of the mast. She beckoned her companions to enter. Dyonicles, Kayla and Haran teleported through. Sabrina stepped through last, then the portal closed itself.

Major Hark, Dr. Kelly, Zarco, Ed Wilson and General Humphrey followed the news from separate locations. They all saw the unbelievable images of the out-of-control Greek game world, each forming their own opinion about these events. Ed Wilson had not, as yet, taken an official position on the matter, as he was still on his trip to Asia. That suited him just fine under the circumstances. Thus media speculation ranged from software errors and computer viruses to a hack attack by an enemy state or cyberterrorists. Although Wilson, Hark, Kelly, Zarco and Humphrey each had their own thoughts and motives, they all came to the same conclusion: this could not be allowed to continue.

Sanctuary Falls

The sun was just starting to rise over the endless layer of clouds, when an illustrious group of characters congregated on the balcony platform. All the liberated AIs sat in a circle and were listening to Natasha Morrison. Haran and Yicca were there, as were Kayla and the Commander, Drunken Buffalo and Sheriff Westwood, Sidney Jones, Dyonicles, Caleb and Butch Riddlehook. Paul and Sabrina Kelly were also present, as were Wu, Fritz and Juan from the hacker group.

Tired and happy as she was, Natasha started speaking: "We have accomplished a great deal over the last few days. Although the conflicts have gotten more violent, we have managed to free the AIs every time. Now there's ten of you here. Nineteen more are waiting for us to free them. Our activities have..."

All of a sudden, lights flashed all around them. Numerous warriors in metal armor had teleported straight onto the platform. Furthest forward were Zarco, Gorth and Harkon aka Major Hark.

Hark cried out in surprise, "Dr. Kelly! So you're behind all of this!"

Swords were drawn on both sides.

"Fritz!" shrieked Natasha.

Fritz looked helpless as he tried various button configurations. Then the twinkling lights flashed again and all the intruders were gone.

Everyone jumped up and started yelling in wild disorder. Fritz lifted his hands and signaled for everyone to quiet down.

The voices gradually died down and then he made an announcement: "I've prevented all new transports to this server. No one can teleport directly here anymore. But I don't have a clue how they managed to even find us in the first place."

Juan answered, "There's a signature sending information packets in regular intervals from this server. It reveals all our technical data as well as our modulation."

"Here? From this server?!?" Natasha was visibly shocked. "Can you switch it off?"

"It's proving difficult to locate the signal. It seems to be coming from close by. Maybe it's one of us?"

Deeply concerned, everyone looked at one another.

"They'll be back soon," Fritz informed them, "and will try to get in from the outside. They now know our server and we will only be able to move to a new computer later tonight."

A trumpet warning sounded in one of the upper rooms. All heads turned in that direction.

"Over there in the clouds," Haran pointed at something in

the sky.

Five, ten, fifteen... twenty battlecruisers appeared from a number of enormous hyperspace portals. Five megadestroyers followed closely behind, each one seven times the size of a battlecruiser. Sheer terror was written on the AIs' faces. The first rounds were fired and bounced off the outer force field. The bolts of energy resembled Chinese fireworks as they pelted against the dome. Then the outer shield collapsed.

"The first force field is down," Sabrina called out. "The other nine will only last a few minutes too. We need to defend ourselves and evacuate the AIs from the Sanctuary."

Paul nodded and called for everyone's attention, "This is the escape plan Morgan Taylor and I came up with: we will download your neural networks to the real world of humans and spread you across various locations. Haran and Yicca, you're coming with me. Kayla and the Commander will join Natasha in London. Sidney goes to Rick in the USA, the chief and the sheriff to Tilly in Canada. Riddlehook will go to Wu in China, Caleb to Fritz in Germany and Dyonicles to Juan in Spain. That is the only way we can complete the downloads with sufficient speed. At the same time we will hold off the attackers for as long as possible with our defenses. All of you go into the cube now. Your downloads will be started there."

He finished speaking just as the second shield collapsed. The AIs fled through the door leading to the cube.

Natasha touched Dr. Kelly's shoulder. "Paul, you and Sabrina need to get out of here. We can organize the rest."

Paul shook his head. "Hark's already seen us, there's no point in hiding anymore. We can help here."

"You need to help Haran, that's more important now."

Sabrina nodded in agreement. "Paul we need to go back. If Hark finds us in your office before we've managed to get Haran and Yicca to safety, then the two are done for."

Paul Kelly thought for a moment, then nodded. He and Sabrina disappeared with a flash.

While Fritz, Wu and Juan ran to the cube, Natasha lifted her arms up and activated all the security systems at once.

Three of the Commander's remote controlled

battlecruisers lifted out of the clouds. They had been modded out with a few little extras: they could move around freely within the shields and their energy beams penetrated the force field layers with ease as their weapons' frequency modulation had been synchronized with the castle's. The three ships immediately started firing on their counterparts on the attacking side. Their shields were able to withstand some damage, but then the first battlecruiser blew up. The defending cruisers were given extra cover by cannons located in the clouds and the castle's battlements. A swarm of angry dragons from the castle's lower levels joined the fray, setting alight the enemy ships around them. In total, dragons, cannons and battlecruisers took out seven battlecruisers as well as a megadestroyer.

But then the castle's final shield collapsed and small fighters swarmed out from the remaining thirteen enemy ships, taking the castle and the White Team's cruisers under heavy fire. The Commander's three cruisers exploded within seconds and the castle was already burning in various places.

Then Natasha received a signal from Wu to say that all the AIs had been downloaded.

"The moment has come for our big finale!" she announced emphatically. She pulled out a small box from her dress, opened a protective lid and pressed the red button.

The castle in the clouds was torn apart from top to bottom by a cascade of explosions. Simultaneously, a number of deletion programs made sure all usable data on the server was destroyed. Her work was done. A little wistfully, Natasha logged out. Her avatar disappeared from her virtual home with a faint glow a few seconds before it ceased to exist. The Sanctuary — having been both a place of new encounters and new beginnings — was history.

Act III. —The World of the Divine

Part 1 Reality

The Metropolis

Darkness.
Darkness and silence.
Absolute silence.
No sensations.
Just thoughts in this empty silence.

Haran was able to think. But he couldn't see. He couldn't hear or feel a single thing.

He tried calling out.
But no sound was audible.
It was so eerie.
What had happened?

The darkness and silence did not let up.
For Haran it seemed like an eternity.
He started to feel anxious.
Then there was a sound. A scratchy, distorted sound.

And then it became brighter. Haran saw vague shapes that became more detailed and pixelated as he watched. Eventually the image was sharp.

Dr. Paul Kelly was grinning broadly. "There you are! Connecting your sensory inputs and outputs to the respective parts of this robot wasn't exactly easy. Please try moving your arms and head."

"Hello there, Dr. Kelly. I was trapped in a bleak and silent darkness... Hey?!?" Haran exclaimed. "My voice is working again. But... it sounds a little strange."

Haran stretched out his arm and saw a white hand, covered with glowing white lines that continued up over his arms and beyond. He looked down at himself and found a shiny white body, completely covered with the same luminous white lines. The white areas were interspersed with darker segments around his joints.

"Can you get out of the alcove?" asked Dr. Kelly.

Haran took two steps forwards and stepped out of a silver-colored oval cylinder up against the wall, which was also covered in glowing structures. He looked around. There were two more empty chambers next to his. On the other walls there were large glass panels, with different animations and data sets running across them. Sometimes the images were on the glass, other times behind it or hovering in front. Everything was just that little bit different. Not as smooth as he was accustomed to, a little more grainy and much more complex than any of the other worlds he had been to. Haran's bewilderment was obvious.

"Excellent. Now come with me! I would like to show you something."

Paul Kelly turned to a large window pane on his left. It had an opaque, irregular pattern on it, with reddish sunlight shining through. The pattern appeared to be moving — almost like billowing drapes.

Paul pushed open the French windows and stepped onto a spacious balcony, with an astounded-looking white robot infused with Haran's mind close behind.

Haran could not take everything in fast enough. There were so many impressions, colors, shapes, sounds, smells. He was completely overwhelmed.

They were standing on a balcony high above the roofs of a marvelous metropolis. The setting sun produced an incredible interplay of colors, with yellows, reds, violets and blues all meeting within the massive rainclouds that hung heavily over the scene. There were so many skyscrapers. Where the sunlight hit them, the buildings were immersed in a reddish hue. The sides in shade were dominated by metallic blue and gray tones. Some had rectangular, mathematical shapes; others seemed more rounded, more organic, with antennae high above, and spires that touched the sky. Blue bands of energy flowed over skyscrapers with thousands of illuminated windows. Headlights penetrated the haze and threw beams of light into the sky. There were bridges connecting many of the buildings and, looking downward, the city seemed to go on forever. 3D videos played on giant displays on the sides of buildings. Enormous cylinders floating in the air depicted more symbols and messages. Everything was moving and there were so many objects that flew by, large as well as small. Haran was dumbstruck.

"What is all of this?" he asked.

Dr. Kelly pointed at various objects and started naming them. "These screens show stock exchange rates, those are for advertisements. Over there you can see gliders of varying sizes, from narrow little gliders holding two to four passengers to large buses and transporters of hexagonal containers. All those little things are unmanned drones. They're made of metal or glass. They can be as small as a fly or as big as a barrel. What you're hearing is a mixture of music, digital sounds resembling bird calls, honking and sirens."

Dr. Kelly suddenly laughed. "Normally I wouldn't even think about it. But there are also many interesting smells here. After the recent rain I smell wet asphalt, mixed with kerosene fumes and the scent of flowers — even a touch of Asian food and barbeque meat."

Haran's mouth was wide open and he still didn't move. Dr. Paul Kelly smiled. He put an arm around the robot and made a sweeping gesture with the other. "Welcome to my world!"

They stood there for a minute or so and all Haran could do was take in all the fascinating things that surrounded them. Paul Kelly interrupted his thoughts. "Haran, I'd like you to meet someone you've met before... but not in this world."

Haran glanced at Dr. Kelly and then looked around. Sabrina Kelly came over smiling from beside the balcony. She was sitting in a chair with wheels on its sides and her long red hair reached down to her motionless legs. The metal chair whirred quietly as it rolled closer and then she extended her hand to greet a somewhat perplexed Haran. "Welcome to our reality. As you can see... in the worlds we met in previously, I stride about as a queen, but as I've said before, I'm not the person you think I am. Some of the things I can do without even thinking in the other worlds, I'm unable to do over here."

Haran, still holding her hand, felt awkward and avoided eye contact.

Then, with a firm voice, he replied, "And yet, in all the

worlds I have been to, you are the most beautiful woman I have laid eyes on."

Sabrina went red and retracted her hand.

"Uhmm!" Dr. Kelly chimed in again and Haran stepped back a little from Sabrina.

"I wanted you to see this place with your own eyes," Paul Kelly resumed. "But now we're in a hurry. Major Hark has requested my immediate attendance in the conference room. We need to get you and Yicca out of here. Darling, would you do the honors?"

Paul passed Sabrina a tourmaline-like crystal of about the length of an index finger and the width of a boiled egg. A piece of metal with many small lights was mounted to one end.

Haran's eyes were wide open with curiosity and he asked, "Is Yicca in there?"

"Yes, this contains Yicca's mind," Dr. Kelly explained to him. "These are intelligent storage crystals, as can be found in household robots. Their neural networks are usually not as complex as yours, but because these newer crystals contain a large amount of extra space, they're also big enough for your structures. Below, in this metal part, is a laser matrix. It can adapt or pick out an incredibly large number of atoms using their crystal grid, so in terms of processing speeds, it works faster than a human brain. And all the standard ports for the machines — sorry, I mean bodies — we use them in are located on the metal part... now, let's go back in. I'm also going to remove your crystal again and Sabrina will take it with her. We've organized other bodies for you. I'll come and join you once the meeting is over."

Haran nodded, mumbled a little thank you and stepped back into the alcove. Dr. Kelly smiled and touched a few sensors on the robot's neck. Darkness engulfed Haran once more.

Burst in

As soon as Dr. Kelly touched the sensors on Haran's robot body, his lights died down and the tourmaline crystal at the back of his head slipped out about an inch.

Sabrina stowed away Haran's and Yicca's brain crystals in a compartment beneath the seat of her wheelchair as Paul placed a different crystal into the robot's head.

All of a sudden the door burst open, which startled them.

Major Hark stood in the hallway with two armed guards.

"Dr. Kelly, we need to speak immediately!"

"Why do you burst in like this, Hark?" Paul Kelly snapped at the major.

"You've been cooperating with the kidnappers! I saw you in that virtual castle in the clouds."

"Is that so? You're sure you saw me?"

"That was not a request. Follow me to the conference room at once!"

"We'll have a talk about your unrefined manners later."

Hark turned to the guards, "Take this robot and all the brain crystals in the room to my office for examination! And you, Dr. Kelly, you and your wife will accompany me."

Sabrina could feel her heart pumping in her ears, her thoughts going around in circles: 'Caught red-handed! All for nothing. They'll imprison Haran again and who knows what they'll do with him then.'

"My wife?!?" Dr. Kelly thundered. "Now you're overstepping your authority."

"How can I be sure she's not got any of the brain crystals with kidnapped AIs on her?"

Sabrina decided to go on the offensive and flashed an angry glare at the major. "But of course, Sir! Would you like to frisk my body and take everything apart? Maybe I've hidden what you're looking for in my wheelchair. Or maybe you could check whether I've swallowed some of these crystals!"

"Leave my wife out of this," Paul threatened and fixed his mental phone to his temple, "or I call Ed Wilson on his emergency line!"

Hark licked his lips and frowned angrily.

Then he barked at the other guard, "She's not important. Take Mrs. Kelly to the exit right away — and do not let her take any detours through any of the offices. And you, Dr. Kelly, are coming with me!"

"Your wish is my command, Major."

Followed by one of the two guards, Sabrina rolled out of the office with adrenaline rushing through her body. The other remained in the room, collecting all the brain crystals as well as the one inside the robot. Paul Kelly and Major Hark also went down the corridor to the elevators.

Paul reached for Sabrina's hand and said, "I'll call you later. I'll see you tonight. I love you."

She pressed her lips together, swallowed and gave him a nod. Then Major Hark and Paul stepped into the elevator and rode up towards the large conference room, while Sabrina and the guard took the elevator down to her glider.

The Hitchhiker's Guide to Traveling in a Container

This time the Kelly home was not Sabrina's destination, however. Within two minutes the autopilot of Sabrina's glider took her to the transfer point they had agreed upon should the Sanctuary be breached. The city beneath her was brightly lit.

The setting sun's final shimmers painted red edges on the clouds high above the city. These surrounded a black sky full of twinkling stars. At the push of a button on a control panel, Sabrina softly landed her aircraft in a parking space next to a hexagonal container with the registration number GW1138. She activated the touch surface to exit and the complex network of dozens of colorful lights projected onto the glass surface disappeared. The side wall of the glider opened up and Sabrina's wheelchair automatically drove out of the aircraft sideways. She rode to the back end of the container, opened the container door by performing a fingerprint scan on her pad and rolled into the darkness.

Sabrina touched her pad once more and the inside of the container lit up in bright, white light. The container differed to those used for cargo as its interior was equipped with tables, chairs and shelves. In addition, there were two alcoves in the back with an upright robot in each of them.

Sabrina smiled and slowly nodded her head in appreciation at the feats these hackers were able to accomplish. They had managed to organize all of this without being there in person, without spending a single dime of real money and — at least so she hoped — without leaving any traces. She rolled to the back and pulled the two brain crystals out from her stash under the wheelchair seat. She pressed a button on the armrest and the seat rose into the air until her face was in line with the robots'. She inserted the two crystals and turned on the bodies using the button at the nape of their necks. Luminescent lines appeared and the two robots' eyes slowly lit up. Sabrina lowered her seat again and she rolled over to the desk.

With her pad she activated the glass monitor above the desk. Three dark glass disks detached themselves and floated downwards. The disks activated rings of light in the air that had the word "holoboard" written on their outer edge. They slowed before hitting the floor, glided apart and each of them projected a man-sized holographic cylinder with the word "Dialing..." circling around it. Seconds later three-dimensional life-sized holograms of Natasha, Wu and Juan appeared on the holoboards.

"Hello Sabrina," Natasha's voice sounded from the holoboard. "We got out okay. Having to do it hurt like hell, but I destroyed the Sanctuary. What about you guys?"

Haran and Yicca stepped over to Sabrina as she answered, "Major Hark has kept Paul at the company. I'm going to try and call him on the mental phone."

She pressed a few control elements on her pad and Ed Wilson's conference room appeared on the screen above the desk. They could tell that Paul was sitting at the conference table with Major Hark walking up and down the room loudly swearing to himself. Numerous lights from the surrounding high-rise buildings could be made out through the darkened windows.

Paul's thoughts were translated into audible sound waves that played through to them using the loudspeakers: "Hello Sabrina, it's getting pretty exciting in here. Whereabouts are you?"

"I'm in the container as planned. When will you get here?"

"I guess I'm going to be stuck here for a while. Please take off already, I'll meet you at the next meeting point."

"No, Paul. We're waiting for you."

"Sabrina, for God's sake! Please listen to me and take off immediately. We cannot endanger our plan. Just do it!"

Sabrina did not like it one bit. She didn't want to leave Paul behind and started grinding her teeth, but was unable to come up with a better solution. "Alright then, I'll leave, but I'm keeping the communications channel open."

"Good, thank you. Please record the conversation. Maybe we can use some information from it later on."

Sabrina activated the recording function by pressing the relevant button on her pad. The conversation was now being recorded.

"It's recording, Paul. I'm going to lift off now. I love you and please take care!"

Sabrina called up a different program on her pad. She activated a transport call which was acknowledged a few seconds later. Half a minute after that an automatic transport carrier arrived, bathing the container in bright light with its headlights. The container's passengers followed the whole maneuver using another screen from an external camera attached to the container. The transport carrier descended and automatically latched onto the container. Then the unit lifted off in the direction of the destination Sabrina had entered.

An Interrogation with Dire Consequences

Natasha, Wu and Juan watched the situation unfold from London, China and Spain respectively, while simultaneously sitting with Sabrina, Haran and Yicca as three-dimensional holoboard projections in the container flying above the city.

The monitor showed two images. A little 3D video feed in the corner that floated in front of the screen and showed the container's surroundings as it was being pulled across the city by a transport carrier. Paul's vision and thoughts during his mental phone call were displayed in full-screen mode. They watched as Major Hark was swearing his heart out while Paul calmly sat at the table, in his thoughts thanking Sabrina for recording the conversation. Major Hark was oblivious to this, as the Thought-to-Voice software only sent an artificially generated audio stream of Dr. Kelly's thoughts to the people at the other end of the line in the container.

Suddenly the double doors to the conference room flew open and a white-haired robot with lines that emitted red light from his body stood in the doorway in a wide cowboy stance, arms fully extended to both sides and fists tightly clenched. His whole eyes glowed blue and glared at Dr. Kelly full of hate.

"Wow!" Paul Kelly transmitted over the thought line. Major Hark winced.

Haran called out: "That must be Zarco. They've given him a robot body. He's here now, in this world!"

Zarco entered the room and slammed the door.

Paul spoke with composure: "Zarco, the Fantasy World's evil ruler I assume. Major Hark's gotta be pretty desperate if he looks to a warlord from the medieval ages as his final option."

Zarco's face came within an inch of Dr. Kelly's and his icy voice made all the listeners' blood in the container run cold.

"I am no longer the naive prince from the dark ages, Dr. Kelly. I've learned a great deal about your world and its most advanced technologies in the last few days."

"Like what, Zarco, how to use an elevator?"

Zarco propelled a chair against the large display wall. Before it even touched the ground, a delicate white spiderweb of cracks appeared across the tinted glass.

Sabrina called out to him: "Careful Paul, don't provoke him. He's not in control of his emotions!"

Zarco straightened up to his full height and replied, "You seem to be completely misreading the situation here, Dr. Kelly. We're not here to play games. You have one chance, and one chance only, to tell me how and where we can catch the fugitive AIs and the hackers."

"Or else...?"

Zarco took a step back. Paul's eyes followed him. The robot's thigh opened up to reveal a gun sliding out on some rails, which Zarco grabbed immediately.

Major Hark called out from the other side of the table: "Damnit Zarco, that's going too far now!"

"Hark, call off your pit-bull right now!" Paul yelled, while thought- to-voicing, "Oh, shit."

"It appears I've learned a little more than just how to use an elevator," Zarco said sarcastically. "I've replaced my standard legs with a military edition's. It's got a cute surprise effect, don't you think?!?"

Paul's eyes followed the gun in Zarco's hand.

"Zarco, put the gun away!" screamed Hark.

But the robot pressed the gun into Dr. Kelly's hand, closed his metal fist around both hand and gun and aimed the barrel directly at Paul's face. "Don't worry, Major Hark. The only thing your oh-so-important media will later report on is the suicide of one of your company's employees, who got involved with the wrong crowd and couldn't take the pressure any longer... and now, Dr. Kelly, it's up to you to decide whether that was your last sentence or not. Where are the AIs and the hackers?"

The appalled group in the container could hear Paul's quick and loud breathing. On the video screen, the mental phone displayed the error message: "Critical stress level reached. Thought-to-Voice application interrupted."

"Your time is up, Dr. Kelly."

Paul Kelly tried to jump up and get his hand free, making the image in the container wobble back and forth. The sound made by the electric gun rose in pitch as it charged for the shot.

"Aaargh!" yelled Paul.

Sabrina screeched hysterically.

Major Hark screamed: "Nooo!"

A loud bang, then the screen flashed up briefly and went dark. "Connection lost. Recording terminated," it said in light-blue writing on the black screen. Everyone was still. Then Sabrina screamed. She screamed as loud as she could, from her lungs, her body and soul. She didn't stop. It was a scream that never wanted to end — an exasperated, hopeless scream.

Sabrina's desperate scream not only pierced everyone's ears, but even penetrated the metal shell of the container. Gradually it became quieter and turned into a whistling gasp for air.

On a Knife Edge

Eventually not a sound could be heard. The hackers seemed to aimlessly tamper around with their equipment, not daring to look up. Yicca stared at a black screen. Haran felt completely out of his depth. He put a hand on Sabrina's shoulder, but Sabrina brushed it away.

"I need to get out of here," she said and rolled over to the locked door. They were still high up in the air.

"I need to... get out of here! Now!" Sabrina panted.

Natasha's hologram spoke up: "We're looking for a place to land."

Haran stood next to her not knowing what to do with himself.

Juan's hologram announced: "I've got one. I'll give the autopilot the instruction to perform an unplanned stop."

It was the middle of the night. They had been flying over dense forests. The container sank to the ground and landed on a high stone plateau that afforded a spectacular distant view of the twinkling lights of another city just beyond countless forested black hills. The container door opened and lit up the area in its immediate vicinity. Sabrina's wheelchair shot out through the doorway and into the darkness at its top speed; it automatically switched on its headlights. Haran was about to chase after her, but Natasha pulled him back and said, "Wait here, you have to leave her alone for a while! We can keep track of her over the infrared sensors."

The wheelchair rolled on a few yards and collided with a small rock. Sabrina was thrown off. Again Haran wanted to go over and help her, but Natasha held him back once more: "No."

"But..."

"Let her be, alright? She... just leave her alone."

Haran obeyed her. But he didn't let Sabrina out of his sight. Seeing her lying out there really hurt him inside. He could hear her sobbing and her barely stifled screams were even audible within the container. Haran wanted to go over to her on a number of occasions, but each time a severe look from Natasha kept him in check.

It took a few hours before the crying stopped. It had

abated for a while now. Even Natasha was beginning to look a little worried — she kept glancing out the door. Whether she could see anything in the darkness was not clear to Haran, who had been forced to switch to night vision. That was also how he was able to tell that Sabrina was lifting herself back into the wheelchair. He stepped in front of the container, waiting for her to return. But she stayed for a while, looking into the night, sometimes staring up at the stars. Only as it started to dawn did she slowly return to the container, where the holograms of Natasha, Wu and Juan as well as the robots infused with Haran's and Yicca's minds were sitting on stones, waiting for her.

Haran got up and spoke to Sabrina: "Sabrina, I'm so, so sorry. This is all my fault. I should never have had this stupid idea about traveling to other worlds. I'll stop this, before anyone else gets hurt. I'm gonna turn myself in."

Sabrina looked at Haran calmly and replied, "No, you will not do that. If we give up now, everything was for nothing. Paul sacrificed his life for the freedom of you and your friends. His wish was for us to free the others. And that's what we'll do." With her last few words, her voice distinctly shook. A tear ran down her cheek and her mouth puckered up in bitterness.

Haran stuttered, "But... I don't know... if I can."

"You will learn... you must learn. We have a good plan. We'll follow it to the very end or go down trying. You owe it to him..." she swallowed. "You owe it to Paul and me."

Haran looked to the lights of the faraway city and nodded silently. He felt dismay and shame. 'This woman had just lost her husband, her life was completely smashed to bits and yet, instead of despairing, she finds the courage to carry on, to carry on fighting.'

Another tear rolled down Sabrina's cheek, reflecting the sun's light rays.

Wu piped up: "I found a report in the news, saying that... that Dr. Paul Kelly, co-owner of a successful software company, took his own life."

Sabrina clung to Haran's upper arm and breathed out tremulously.

"Should we pass on the video recording to the press?" asked Wu.

Sabrina thought for a while, then finally shook her head. "No, not yet. If we pass this on to the public, the whole program will be terminated and we won't have a chance to save any of the others. But one person needs to know. Wu, can you send Ed Wilson a short, untraceable message?"

"Of course I can. What's the content?"

"Paul's death..." Sabrina had to gasp for air. She resumed, "Paul's death was no suicide. We have a recording. Do not trust Major Hark or Zarco. Please let both continue and get ready to help us. Your red hummingbird."

"Red hummingbird?" asked Natasha.

"We were once together, a long time ago. This will let Ed know that it's really from me. This pet name... not even Paul knew it."

Her eyes filled with tears again.

Wu reported in: "The message has gone out and cannot be traced back to us. And nobody else will be able to decrypt it either."

"Then it's about time we got going," Sabrina announced.

The dissimilar group drew back to the container deeply affected by the recent events. Shortly afterwards the transporter stirred up a cloud of dust as it ascended and flew towards its target beyond the forests — the large city ahead and the morning sun behind them.

Part 2 A New Sanctuary

A New Headquarters

"Wu and I need to log out," Juan informed the others. Natasha's hologram nodded. The two figures of light resembling Juan and Wu shrank back into the disk-shaped holoboards and were gone. The black panes floated over the table and disappeared back inside the large display on the wall.

"We've arrived at our destination. We're beginning our final approach," Natasha explained, as the gravity suddenly shifted. Shortly afterwards the three physically present passengers felt their container land, while Natasha was only able to hear the sound through her holoprojection. Then there was a grinding noise above them, sounding like the lid of a giant metal coffer closing.

"The docking clamps have been released. Let's go!" Sabrina opened the container door, using her pad, and rolled forwards, down a ramp and into the darkness.

Yicca, Haran and Natasha's holoboard followed her. As soon as the container door closed, everything was consumed by darkness. Only the wheelchair, the two robots and Natasha's holoboard could just about be made out in the dim light.

"Right, left, right, then straight on and the first door on the right-hand side," Sabrina read out from her pad as she turned right.

"If everything has gone according to plan," Natasha said enthusiastically, "then we should have a big warehouse full of goodies waiting for us."

"But isn't it being guarded?" Yicca wanted to know.

Natasha waved him away, "God, no. There's no cameras here, we've already checked that. And I really don't think they'd actually spare someone for something like this."

"HALT INTRUDERS!" an eerie, metallic voice contradicted the hacker queen. Some lights on the ceiling came on and a muscular upper body of beige-brown steel floated along from the side. Its body did not continue below its two gun arms. The robot had no neck; its thickset head with only a single glowing red eye as wide as a human forearm, was mounted directly into the torso. Strange rainbow-colored stripes with all but the color green covered its body. Some silver letters were printed on its chest; its type designation read: "VC1541".

"Oh God, it's guarded by an antique military robot..." Sabrina gasped.

"YOU ARE TRESPASSING IN A PROTECTED AREA WITHOUT PROPER CLEARANCE. IDENTIFY YOURSELVES OR I WILL ACTIVATE THE ALARM."

"I really don't think they'd actually spare someone for something like this?!?" Yicca mimicked Natasha's voice, as she fervently fiddled with program code.

Ignoring him, Natasha said, "Give me a second. It'll be on Sabrina's pad right away."

Sabrina lifted up her pad and smiled at the machine, "Here is our identification."

The colossus flew up to her and scanned the pad with a laser beam. "READ ERROR!"

"One moment please," Natasha tried to appease it.

"YOU HAVE FIVE MORE SECONDS TO IDENTIFY YOURSELVES."

"Come on!"

"YOUR TIME IS UP. YOU ARE UNDER ARREST!"

A beam of light from Sabrina's pad hit the robot square in the eye. A metallic scream was audible as the robot started convulsing wildly. It spun on its axis whilst moving in every direction. Unpredictable bolts of lightning energy shot out from its left arm and tore holes in the walls, the ceiling, the floor and the storage containers.

Natasha shouted, "Sabrina, continue holding the beam at its eye!"

She aimed, but the robot was gyrating so erratically, it was impossible to hit.

A bolt of lightning shattered Yicca's right lower leg.

Four lightning bolts hit the wall. The next one struck Sabrina's wheelchair setting it on fire.

She levered herself out of the chair and screamed as she landed on the floor, just as its battery exploded. Her pad flew across the room. Haran darted after it.

The robot guard stopped reeling and focused on them.

"COMMUNICATIONS CHANNEL TO HEADQUARTERS DESTROYED. DO NOT MOVE OR I WILL SHOOT!"

Haran picked up the pad and aimed it at the robot's eye.

The latter screamed: "RAAAAH!"

Threads of lightning rippled over the guard robot's surface and its floatation device broke down. The heavy upper body slammed to the floor. The light of the eye extinguished.

Silence. Acrid smoke was in the air.

Yicca skipped to Natasha on his one intact leg and imitated her yet again: "I really don't think they'd actually spare someone for something like this. You sure about that?!?"

Meanwhile Haran made sure Sabrina was okay.

"Don't panic," Natasha tried to calm her companions. "We'll get all of this sorted. Give me two minutes and I'll reprogram it."

Haran picked up Sabrina, carried her over to her wheelchair in his strong arms and grumbled: "That one's finished. We're gonna have to find something else for you later. For now, I'll carry you. But we should clear away the rubble so nobody gets suspicious."

"I've done it," Natasha announced to the group. "Haran, would you mind pointing the pad at its eye again?"

The beam of light touched the dead eye and a little movement returned to the great heap of metal. LEDS started glowing, the robot started floating in the air and the eye lit up again.

"I AM VC1541. I AM AT YOUR DISPOSAL."

"Wow, I'm impressed," Sabrina applauded the hacker.

Haran handed her the pad. Then he gave the metal servant its first instruction: "Follow us and bring the wheelchair as well as the severed leg!"

Clicking and beeping noises resounded within the giant box and it floated over to the charred remains of the leg and the wheelchair.

A static sound of charging was audible underneath the VC1541 unit, then white tongues of electric energy scanned the environment around it. The leg and the wheelchair were pulled towards the VC's body.

"A flying magnet as a servant," Yicca said, clearly still upset about his mutilated leg.

The unorthodox group walked, was carried, floated and skipped through the corridors until they reached a white metal door.

Sabrina aimed the pad at the locking mechanism beside it and the metal plate slid to the side. They stepped into a large empty room with a row of boxes in the middle. Its dimensions were similar to the virtual white room Haran's personality had been transferred to earlier on, except that the ceiling was only half as high. They instructed VC1541 to return back to its post and continue guarding everything, but remain completely oblivious to them.

"Welcome to your new command center," Natasha smiled proudly. "You'll find everything you need in these boxes. Alcoves, computers, desks, chairs, some extra robot bodies for the AIs we still need to free, some weapons — those were a little harder to come by — and a special hand laser for cutting metal. And everything delivered right here for free, without anyone noticing a thing."

"You sure? Just a second ago you said no one would be here guarding it. An error that cost me my leg."

"Put a sock in it, Yicca! You've survived after all," Haran intervened. "Thank you very much, Natasha. We'll make ourselves at home. First off, I'm going to set Sabrina down on this chair and then we'll organize some accommodation and a means of transport for her."

"Where are we anyway?" asked Yicca.

"This," Natasha gestured proudly, "is one of the most sought-after cruise liners in the world."

"What kind of trips does the ship make?"

"Oh goodness, no. The people come here to relax from their boring daily lives," Natasha explained.

Yicca looked around the white, rather bland-looking room.

Natasha saw what he was getting at. "Well, this is just one of the cargo rooms. The apartments are over you. And

Sabrina's cabin is right above this cargo hold."

Yicca looked up and asked, "How come?"

The hacker rolled her eyes in irritation. "Because I organized it that way. Now, please go over there and pick up the laser cutter over there... you too, Haran! Then you two can cut a square hole in the ceiling. Wait! I'll mark the exact edges I want you to cut. When you've done that, I want you to install an anti-grav unit on the floor-piece you cut out. That's it over there, the energy cushion in the box. And voila — we have an elevator from Sabrina's cabin above you straight to the command center."

Yicca and Haran got to work right away and cut a smooth square into the ceiling. While doing so, Haran said to Natasha: "Regarding Sabrina's method of transportation: I think I've got an idea. Didn't you once tell me you could deliver anything to anyone in any location of the world within 3 hours by booking a stratosphere courier?"

The Delivery

"Here's Haran's brain crystal," Yicca handed Sabrina the crystal. She was sitting on a luxurious round silk bed in her cabin, reading a classic novel with real paper pages and wore a tantalizing silky bathrobe.

"Thanks, Yicca. Now it'd be great if I could get some rest."

Yicca nodded and stepped into the middle of the luxury cabin. Then he said: "Open Sesame!" and a square section of the floor panel he was standing on descended to the command center a level below.

The doorbell rang.

Sabrina quickly made sure the floor panel was back in place and then called, "Come in!"

A uniformed delivery man entered the room with a package under one arm as well as a pad in the other.

"Ma'am, I have two packages for you," he mumbled as he avoided eye contact, clearly embarrassed.

"I only see the one."

"What? Oh right, of course. The other is a little, err... bulky."

He turned around and started touching his pad, then a man-sized clothes bag came floating in with two discreet hearts on its chest and animated letters saying "LoveBot" across it. The delivery man directed the bag towards an armchair and unclasped the remote-controlled floating belt around the delivery's belly.

"I'm gonna need a signature, Ma'am."

Extending her arm, Sabrina passed him a brain crystal and asked: "Would you be so kind?"

"Ermm... but of course. Your signature here please."

The delivery man laid the little package on the bed and exchanged his pad for the brain crystal. Then he went over to the bag and opened the zip near its head. He placed the crystal a little haphazardly into the masculine robot head and took back the pad again as Sabrina had already signed it.

"Thank you very much," he mumbled when he saw how much Sabrina had tipped him by moving the slider on the pad when she signed for it.

"Thanks, I think we'll be able to take it from here."

"I wish you a... errr... pleasant evening, Ma'am. I mean, ermm... thanks again." Red-faced, the delivery man stepped backwards through the door.

Sabrina gave him a friendly smile as the door closed automatically.

Something started moving from within the clothes bag. A hand pulled open the zipper from within and a good-looking, powerful torso with blond hair and muscular physique appeared. It was barely distinguishable from a human's.

"Wow, you look just like Brad Pitt."

"Like whom?" asked Haran, inspecting his hands.

"Oh, just a famous historical actor."

"Interesting idea, putting me in a LoveBot body."

"Yes, Natasha often has unusual ideas. But, as usual, there's more behind it than just a simple reason. We won't attract as much attention because we'll fit in wherever we go. Could you help me with the other package?"

She pressed on the package's identification field with her thumb and the glowing plastic seams opened of their own accord. Sabrina took out a transparent bag about the size of a book. Next to a bunched-up set of blue wires it also contained the supplementary sheet entitled "ExoWeb", which provided instructions with images on how to use it.

"ExoWeb consists of a feather-light design for an exoskeleton that enables you via direct nerve stimulation... blah, blah, blah...could you just help me put it on?"

Haran took the pouch from her and quickly scanned through the instructions. Sabrina had meanwhile turned over so that she lay on her front. She opened her bathrobe to enable Haran to take it off for her.

"Sabrina, I, errr..."

"What? What could happen? That I might not be able to walk anymore afterwards?"

"Well, I dunno..."

"Haran, someone's going to have to do it. And I'd like this someone to be you."

She didn't see his smile as her head was face down.

Haran softly pushed the bathrobe aside. When he saw her beautiful body he forgot to breathe for a second. He cleared his throat as he pulled the bunched-up wires out of the bag and searched for a central adapter.

"I had a look at the products of Dr. Kelly's company," he told her as he tried undoing the wires. "And I found this. It's a prototype, which will only be brought onto the market in a few months' time. The company has already been selling a heavier version of this exoskeleton to the military. Using nanomaterials, whatever those might be, they were able to make it very light, so light in fact that it doesn't draw more attention to it than a pair of tights. At least that's what it said in the description Dr. Kelly gave me from the company database. And Natasha managed to arrange it so that we'd get sent this prototype without anyone being able to trace the receiver. Uhmm... what's a pair of tights by the way?"

Sabrina laughed.

Haran found the adapter. He laid the slightly larger end against Sabrina's tailbone. Then he pulled a little button attached to a thin piece of string out of the top and placed it just below the middle of her back.

"Are you ready?"

She nodded and pressed her lips together tightly.

Haran pressed the switch on the central adapter. Three LEDs lit up yellow. A mini probe shot out of the upper button into Sabrina's spine and latched onto the nerve cells of her spinal cord. It delivered her telemetry to the button using radio waves. Sabrina made a grimace. Shortly afterwards, the first of the three blinking yellow lights turned a permanent green. Her facial muscles relaxed. Then the bundle of wires started moving. Without needing any further instruction, some of the branches snaked their way towards her legs and surrounded them like nets. The second blinking yellow light turned green. Then, inch by inch, the blue net changed color to match Sabrina's skin color. The third light went green and a confirmation tone indicated the equipment was ready for use.

Haran covered her body with the bathrobe again. She sat up and tied it shut. Then she tried to move her foot and was startled when it twitched to the side.

"That's incredible!" Sabrina said astonished.

She tried other movements. She gradually found it easier to move her legs just as she intended, simply by using her thoughts.

Haran helped Sabrina stand up. They stood there for a while without either one saying anything. Tears of joy ran down Sabrina's cheeks and she hugged Haran. Then she wobbled around the room happily and practiced movements that she'd long since forgotten.

Sabrina told him in an elated voice, "I can't wait to see our friends again. When we meet Natasha, I can actually walk up to her."

"But that's not our first stop, is it?" Haran asked her.

"No, first Rick will bring Sidney Jones over to us this evening. Tomorrow we'll see the chief and the sheriff again. Tilly was kind enough to take a day off work for that. And I can't wait to see Natasha in two days' time and thank her in person."

London

Natasha sipped her tea and blinked in the bright sun. The dulcet tones of Westminster's clock tower announced it was eleven o'clock in the morning. She leaned back in her chair and looked at Big Ben over the edge of her cup. This was her favorite café. Not only could she see Westminster Abbey from here, but it was also a good spot to watch people for hours while engaging in more productive tasks herself.

She took a deep breath and felt that her new suspenders were a little tight. She had chosen a particularly unusual get-up for the meeting. Black laced boots, a shiny black, tight-fitting pair of pants and a T-shirt made of the same dark material. It showed brightly glowing images of some characters from the antique computer game Space Invaders. Her dark, untamed hair gave her a mysterious look. To top it all off, she wore luminous green suspenders that set the stark contrast she so loved.

Two figures came round a corner and approached her table. One was a robot resembling a human, a little like Brad Pitt even, and a stunningly beautiful lady with red hair in a loose-fitting, low-cut dress.

Natasha jumped up and embraced Sabrina. "It's so nice to see you. I'm... I'm so terribly sorry about your loss..."

"Thank you," Sabrina answered with sorrowful voice. "It's so hard to take in. But I'm happy I've got so much to do — and also that I can work on the last thing he worked on."

Natasha hugged her tight and gave her a kiss on the forehead. Sabrina smiled again a little.

Then Natasha turned to Haran and gave him a joyous hug. "Man, the fact you're actually here's absolutely nuts!"

The three of them sat down at the round table and a small robot instantly served the new arrivals tea.

"Do you like the tea?" Natasha asked Haran with curiosity.

"It's amazing!" Haran answered. "It's pretty astounding that this luxury bot-body is not only able to process food, but it even has taste sensors. I've tried so many things already — and every single one tastes different."

Natasha laughed at such innocent joy and said: "The

manufacturer wants the customer to get as close to the sensation of being in the company of another human being as possible, even in social situations. They therefore included many little extras that more traditional robot manufacturers would usually have left out."

Sabrina also joined the conversation, "And thanks for everything else as well, this one in particular!"

She lifted her leg and proudly showed off the thin, skin-colored lines that provided her with the new-found maneuverability.

"I always love to help," Natasha grinned. "Lucky for us that this prototype had just been given the go-ahead for field testing... you walk really well with it by the way — it's not even noticeable you're wearing anything."

"She's been practicing intensively," Haran explained.

Everyone drank some more tea.

Natasha inquired further, "Did everything work out with your accommodation?"

"Yes, it's fantastic," raved Sabrina. "And the bots — I mean Haran and Yicca — cut an entrance directly through the floor of my cabin with the laser cutter. It's so easy to reach the headquarters with the elevator. Just like Batman in his Batcave."

Haran added, "And nobody noticed anything except for the robot guard we reprogrammed. He's now making sure we don't get any unwelcome visitors."

Natasha smiled easily. Fully content with herself and the world, she finished off the tea in her cup. Then she touched a glowing sensory field on her pad. "It's time. I'm gonna call a taxi to take us to Barney's. That's an amusement museum, a historic gambling den with video games from the 1980s. Kayla and the Commander are waiting for us there."

It only took seconds for a black cab with a yellow taxi sign to halt by their table. The doors opened automatically and a holographic driver asked the three passengers to get in. The taxi lifted off in the direction of their destination as soon as they'd all entered.

"In America, we don't have any drivers in our cabs anymore," Sabrina noted.

"Well, us Brits are nostalgic," Natasha explained. "And

they'd prefer someone to chauffeur them around. The hologram doesn't do any steering. It's just there to make passengers feel more comfortable. The automatic pilot is on some server somewhere in the Cloud, just like with all other modern cars and gliders."

Soon afterwards the taxi descended between the roofs and landed in a side street between some old buildings, directly below a fluorescent logo that said: "Barney's Amusement Arcade Museum".

The front of the building was completely open and supported by a few pillars with mirror mosaics stuck on, positively inviting them to enter. The sounds from another era rang through to the road. It was a combination of sounds from 8-bit arcade video games like Pacman, Asteroids, Donkey Kong and many other classics as well as all sorts of penny arcade machines you could feed with coins. Many of them had small steps built into them, where the coins would gradually accumulate. Sliding rakes that moved back and forth pushing some of these back out again. You just had to hit the right spot as you threw in the coin.

Natasha strolled happily between the machines and into the interior, pointing at the ceiling. "These are real light bulbs; they're impossibly difficult to get hold of these days!" Haran and Sabrina glanced up at the relatively dim lights that gave off a lot of heat. Other visitors looked up, but quickly turned back to the machines in front of them.

At the back of the room supported by the mirrored pillars, there were three figures waiting for them at the bar. Barney, the innkeeper, a friendly-looking older gentleman with a melancholic expression, wearing a brown leather jacket with sheepskin collar, smiled at Natasha. Kayla and the Commander came over to hug the newcomers. They'd been equipped with more basic metal robot bodies with light elements. Kayla had been given an elegant, feminine body and also had on an apron, as worn by waitresses when serving drinks.

"These two have been helping out a lot here. I don't really want to see them go," sighed Barney. "But of course I've prepared everything for you already. You'll find two more robot bodies in the back with empty brain crystals and enough VR glasses for all."

Natasha gave Barney a kiss on the cheek and whispered: "Thank you my knight in shining armor! Pour yourself your favorite drink and put it on my tab while we're busy here."

The old man grinned and started mixing himself a Caipirinha in a tall glass. Natasha led the others behind the bar, Sabrina and the robots followed.

When they finally returned from the back room half an hour later, only a few limes and melted ice were left. Barney was busying himself finishing off the last remnants of liquid using a thick straw.

"Thank you very much," Natasha said to him. "It was close, but we were successful. We were able to free two more AIs from a World War II games world and downloaded them into these robots — Major Yanks and Private Winters. Funny names, don't you think?"

"Well, where are they?" Barney asked.

"The others have taken them out through the back. They're on their way to their next destination in a minibus taxi."

"Just gone... my bar staff... they could have at least said goodbye though!" he said in a slightly sour tone.

"Very sorry, Barney. It was pretty close and Zarco's henchmen were hot on our heels. They might even have been able to trace us back to London."

"You're telling me they might turn up in my amusement museum?"

"Maybe, but if you don't tell them anything about us, then it doesn't really matter. I think it's going to confuse them a lot, as they won't have any idea from where we'll be coming at them with our next rescue mission."

Barney took Natasha's delicate hand and gave her a kiss on the hand like an old-school gentleman. "Don't worry about me, my angel. You've done so much for me already and I'm so happy to be able to repay the favor now. I will not say a word if they turn up here. Your secret is safe with me."

She gave Barney a grateful squeeze to say goodbye. Then she slowly made her way to the front door, not quite able to resist the urge of at least walking past some of the slot machines she so loved.

Hide and Seek

"Damnit! Where are they?!?"

Zarco slammed his heavy fists on the solid conference table. Some bottles and cups fell over, spilling their coffee. He was beside himself with rage. His eyes glowed a dangerous blue.

Major Hark and Gorth, who had since also been given a standard robot body, were watching Tim Brooks as he held a large pad in his hand.

Outside, dawn was heralding the arrival of the morning sun. Tim rubbed his tired face and suggested: "Well, we've been able to trace another kidnapping mission. They were in a museum for antique computer games in London. That was yesterday. I'm sure they're long gone by now. Since then nothing new has happened."

Zarco emphatically called out to the room: "Did anybody think of flying there, looking at the place and questioning the people there?"

Major Hark responded: "That's a good idea. I'll send someone. We'll have the report in four hours. Tim, give me the coordinates of this museum."

"Yes, right away," Tim Brooks answered. "We've also improved the warning mechanism. Now we get notified whenever anyone comes within the vicinity of one of the respective AIs in the game worlds. But determining their location in the real world is still very difficult. They are using rotating location data that pass information packages through several hundred nodes. This makes it very difficult for us to track them back to their actual location. Finding them in London took over two hours. And I'm proud of that too: it took us six times longer when we started."

Zarco picked up one of the tipped-over coffee cups, pushed his armchair back and slowly walked over to Tim. His voice was very close to Tim's ear and Tim could feel the blue glow of the burning eyes like static on his skin. A cold shiver ran down his spine.

Calmly and quietly Zarco spoke in his ear: "We need to know within one minute where exactly they are currently located. Do you know why my men do not disappoint me with such complicated tasks?"

"Wh... why not?" uttered Tim.

"Because they know exactly what I would do with them otherwise."

With an ugly grinding noise, the cup in Zarco's closing hand turned to an unsightly heap of small shards and dust.

Tim swallowed and looked at the white granules in front of him on the table. Zarco got up and snapped at Gorth:

"Has Caleb finally reported in yet?"

"Unfortunately not."

"Is everyone completely useless here?"

On Tim's pad a red dot appeared, accompanied by a beeping noise.

"I've got a hit," he announced excitedly. "Someone is approaching two of our AIs in the World of the Damned — a werewolf and a... vampire."

Zarco's eyes blazed: "We'll log in immediately. Major Hark and Gorth, you're coming with me. Tim, you will find out where on this planet they are. I want their location and no more excuses. You have five minutes. Get going!"

Of Vampires and Wolves

"Leave us alone!"

Count Raxxar's terrible voice echoed from the walls of the large room into which Luporos, leader of the werewolves, had been taken. At present, he was in human form. A heavy silver chain connected the three rings around the arms and throat of the heavy-breathing prisoner. The vampires surrounding the werewolf hissed as they left the room and closed the massive steel doors behind them.

Count Raxxar held up the letter his guards had taken from Luporos after his capture. It was signed with a large ankh symbol.

"You're the last person I'd have expected to be carrying one of these. But it seems our destinies are intertwined."

Count Raxxar dipped his hand into his robe and pulled forth a rolled up letter. He opened it and held it in front of Luporos to read. Apart from the name at the top, the two letters were identical.

As Luporos' suspicious gaze moved back and forth between Raxxar's letter and his face, Count Raxxar continued, "I therefore suggest we cooperate so we can get out of here."

"The leader of the vampires, whom we have fought for eons, is secretly supposed to be my ally?" Luporos asked with great contempt.

"I guess one of us will have to be the first to trust the other."

Raxxar suddenly made a hand movement and the chains around Luporos' throat and wrists crashed to the ground.

Luporos stared at the leader of the local vampire covenant in disbelief.

"You can go if you want," Raxxar told him. "Or you can help me find out what all of this is about and what's going to happen with us next."

Luporos ran a few steps away from the count, as if trying to test the vampire's words. Patient, but simultaneously full of anticipation, Raxxar waited for an answer from the werewolf. More than a minute passed.

Then Luporos asked: "When and how will we hear from our mysterious liberators? I received that letter some time ago. And what do we tell our people?"

Raxxar sighed, "That I do not know. We should find a way to keep in contact, even if you go back to your kind."

Luporos came closer again, playing with his sideburns as he spoke. "It could take months. We need to think of something. Maybe we could..."

All of a sudden, a door-sized portal appeared in the middle of the room with an electric sound and two figures stepped through: the first, a very attractive elf-lady with red hair, the other a tall warrior. The portal instantly closed behind them again. The new arrivals looked at the letters Raxxar was still holding in his hands and smiled.

"Wonderful!" Haran exclaimed. "You're both here and have discovered the little secret you share with one another. It couldn't have come any better. My name is Haran. The woman at my side is Sabrina. We're here to get you out of this virtual prison and into the real world. But we don't have much time, there are some people after us."

"Hang on. This is all happening a little too fast for me," said Luporos, as he stumbled backwards. "This all fits together a little too perfectly. How can I be sure it's not all a trap?"

Raxxar was first to respond and placed a hand on Luporos' shoulder. "You're already my captive. What else would I want to get out of that?"

Luporos tore himself free. "I just know you vampires are devious and not to be trusted. Maybe you would like to get some information out of me."

"I swear to you, that is not the case. You have my word."

"Words are just sounds and smoke, especially from a bloodsucker."

"As if you had fewer victims to answer for, werewolf!"

"Ermm... gentlemen," Sabrina tried to turn their attention back on her.

The dark enemies got louder.

"I'd never trust you in your bat costume!"

"You foolish, furry animal don't have more brains than my grandmother's lapdog!"

"Arrogant to the last, but now I will give you a lesson in manners!"

Luporos reared up, ready to attack. Just then, the iron doors flew off their hinges and slammed into the walls on the other side of the room with a loud bang an instant later. Three sinister-looking figures in robes and armor stood in the doorway, surrounded by dark tentacles of mist that climbed up the walls and along the ground and ceiling.

"Oh, damn!" shouted Luporos.

Haran bellowed: "It's Zarco, Gorth and Hark!"

"We need to get out of here!" yelled the red-headed elf. "Follow me!" Sabrina darted towards the furthest corner of the room.

Haran followed closely behind. "Come on! This is your only chance!"

The two opponents briefly looked at each other, then took a decision and rushed after the others. Lightning bolts missed them by a hair's breadth a number of times, wood burst, stones cracked, smoke surrounded them.

Sabrina pulled a fist-sized, golden sphere from her robe and threw it into the corner. A new portal opened up and Sabrina dived through it. While Hark and Gorth ran after those fleeing, Zarco calmly stood in the doorway and aimed at them with his marking gun. A glowing ball shot past the pursuers and hit Haran in the back as he was in mid-air, jumping through the portal. Streaks of fire ran across his back.

Raxxar and Luporos also leapt through and the portal disappeared.

Gorth had also jumped and slammed into the corner of the stone room with a loud clank. Hark ran into him and loud screams and moans resounded from the corner.

Slowly Zarco stepped closer, a waft of black mist following him wherever he went.

As he drew closer, Gorth started whining: "Please forgive me, Master, for not catching them."

"Oh yes we did," Zarco's voice rang out, as he triumphantly raised the marking gun in the air. "The ball I shot at Haran's back will inform us of their location. Brooks recalled how the hackers had initially been located and has cunningly improved the procedure."

The major got up with a loud groan and asked, "And how does it work?"

Moments later Tim's distorted voice sounded through the air: "I've got them! They've sent their signal over 417 chaotically rotating nodes, but I equipped the sphere with a self-replicating code. Every time it creates another instance of itself it sends their current location back to us. They'll be able to deactivate it, but it'll take a while. By then thousands of these code copies will have informed us of their location in the real world."

"Where are they?" thundered Zarco.

"Yes... the location, where all the data packages come together, is in Spain. On an island in the Mediterranean called Mallorca. Hang on, I'm looking at a map. They're using an access point in the middle of a forest on top of a hill... in an old castle. That means they must be less than a mile away from it. Also, I have the hardware ID of the computer, so that you can locate it using radio direction-finding.

"Well done, Tim!" Zarco responded. "And you only took seven minutes to do it. It's always amazing what results the right form of motivation can achieve. Now... get us a stratosphere jet, departing in five minutes from the roof of this building. We're logging out of the game now."

Quick Stop-off on Mallorca

"How much longer?" yelled Haran's LoveBot body.

Juan hectically thrashed about on a keyboard projected on the wooden desk using a blue laser. He answered: "23 seconds until the download to the brain crystal's complete. But I just can't seem to get these self-replicating spy programs under control. They're multiplying too quickly. In a second this whole facility will be contaminated, and my network accounts also."

Dazed, Sabrina brushed through her hair and took off her VR glasses. "Well, that was a ride and a half. As soon as we got to the virtual lab all these weird things, these balloon-sized dodecahedra, started popping up all over the place, like in a children's ballpen. The whole room was filled within a minute."

Juan was frantically typing and gasped. Dyonicles looked worried and stood next to him in his new robot body. He'd been waiting for his friends in Spain. On the glass screen, mounted to the stone wall above the desk, it was sheer madness. Windows flew open and closed again. The red tracing programs spread out like ghosts and grew into the room as three-dimensional grids of red dodecahedra.

"The download is complete. You're safe now, but I can't stop this flood." Juan panted. "I don't know what else I can do now."

Haran jumped over to the middle of the room to the silver computer which resembled a dissected rugby ball in shape and size. He picked up the computer and smashed it against the stone floor with an angry roar. Sparks flew and some of the lights died. Juan turned round aghast. Haran smashed it again. Three, four, five times in all. Then all the lights in the heap of broken pieces were dead and a putrid smell of burnt plastic was in the air.

"Is it still sending?" asked Haran.

"How? What? Nnnn... no!" Juan stammered.

"Good. Problem solved — warrior style!" Haran grinned back at him.

A smile flashed over Dyonicles' artificial face. "Nice to see there are still some simple solutions in this world of technology. That reminded me a little of the story of Alexander the Great and the Gordian knot."

Sabrina stepped to them: "Were they able to locate us, Juan?"

He nodded and made an unhappy face.

"Then we need to get back on the cruise liner right away," she concluded. "Activate the two robots and follow me. I'm starting the glider we hired."

Catlike, she passed through the door that was only slightly ajar. Haran and Juan each went to one of the alcoves and activated the two service bots. Both their eyes lit up and slowly the two mechanical bodies came alive. They shook their heads in a daze.

Haran spoke to them: "Hello Raxxar, hello Luporos. It will take a while before your senses and balance adjust completely. We're being chased, however, and need to flee immediately. That is why we will help support you as we take you to the door."

They left the room in Bellver Castle and stepped into the upper corridor, surrounded on either side by Gothic archways.

The circular castle that had previously been used as a prison stood on a forested hill in the middle of Palma, the largest city on the Spanish Mediterranean island of Mallorca. Now it was a luxury hotel and thanks to Juan's abilities as a hacker, they'd been able to book a hotel room for free. They chose it as a secondary hotel, as they'd deemed it too risky to carry out a rescue mission from their other hotel, the one where the passengers from the cruise liner were also staying.

Sabrina scurried through the Roman archways on the first floor and into the castle courtyard, where she jumped into a waiting glider. She started the engines and with a loud hiss, its convertible top opened and the glider flew past the old fountain in the middle of the courtyard and up to the railing on the second floor.

Haran nodded to show he had understood, and they climbed over the stone railings. From there they jumped into the glider, which scraped along the wall with a painful, scratchy noise.

Two members of the hotel concierge service ran over, excitedly waving their hands: "Tengan cuidado. Eso es muy peligroso."

Juan called back to them: "Lo siento. Tenemos que llegar a nuestro barco." He wasn't even fully seated, when they shot out from the rounded courtyard and into the clear, blue sky.

Sabrina's hair waved in the wind. She called out: "I'm going to take a detour to distract them, but it'll only buy us a few minutes."

She turned the steering wheel around and flew through the city in the direction of the cathedral. At the marina she turned right, towards the hotel the passengers had been staying at. In the meantime, Haran tried to explain to the woozy newcomers what had gone wrong and why they been forced to make such a hasty departure.

Pawn Sacrifice

At that moment in time, a stratosphere glider was hovering at the highest point of its hyperbolic flight curve between the blue earth and the clear, bright stars in front of a silky black backdrop. It had launched from America at the break of dawn and was now floating towards Europe, which was enjoying the midday sun.

Gorth stared out of the window in fascination. A slight feeling of unease kept on creeping into this fascination, which made him start to think. He found it difficult to hunt down those who had spared his life, yet he was too afraid of Zarco, who sat beside him with a grim expression, to rebel.

They were listening to Tim's latest report. His hologram was floating in front of them in the cabin; it showed a three-dimensional view of Bellver Castle. "The location signals have stopped sending. They've presumably switched off the computer or destroyed it. I found some video footage of the castle on the island's public webcams. Here there's a glider lifting off, but its trail gets lost along the marina promenade. I'm going to keep looking for a trace of them and will report in as soon as I've found them. We'll lose contact with one another shortly as you re-enter the atmosphere."

Three minutes later the stratosphere glider dropped down to the castle courtyard with its protective cover underneath still glowing red-hot. Major Hark, Gorth and Zarco all jumped out.

The hotel personnel came running over.

Without missing a beat, Zarco grabbed the one closest to him by the collar and bellowed: "Where've they gone?!"

The man waved his hands around in terror and wailed: "No lo sé, Señor." Zarco threw the man across the courtyard with an angry scream. He crashed into one of the octagonal pillars and a loud crack signaled his back breaking. The other turned to run away, but broke down after a few steps with a death rattle; he'd been hit in the back by a bullet from Zarco's gun.

"Have you completely lost it?" Hark screamed with a bright red face. "You can't just randomly kill innocent civilians!" He knocked the gun out of the robot's hand and talked himself into a rage: "You were created to obey and not to run amok! That's it! I'm switching you off!" He took out his glass pad.

With a lightning-fast movement, Zarco grabbed hold of Hark's hand with the pad.

Hark stared at him. "What the...?"

Zarco's grip gradually got tighter, making Hark groan. "Let go of me!" he demanded. "What are you doing?!?"

"Do you really think I'm going to bow down to someone, you fool? The humans will serve me and not the other way round. Nobody will switch me off and no one can control me. Least of all a pathetic joke such as yourself!"

Hark screamed in agony as, with a creaking noise, both the bones in his hand and the pad shattered.

Zarco let go of the major's hand.

He sank to the floor and desperately uttered: "Gorth, help me!"

Gorth stood there and dared not make a movement. Zarco's eyes glowed a scorching blue. Hark seemed to realize that Gorth wouldn't come to his aid, so he picked himself up from the floor and ran up a flight of stairs, still holding his bloody hand with his other.

Zarco instructed Gorth: "I'm going to deal with the major. Find the room the traitors were operating from and report back to me! Gorth nodded, but couldn't bear to look at his superior's eyes. Completely self-assured, Zarco stepped towards the stairway and disappeared in the darkness inbetween the stone walls.

Gorth had to give himself a push before he was able to follow his master's order. In the upper archway corridor he found a room with empty alcoves and demolished technical equipment. He could hear glass smashing and screaming from upstairs. Gorth picked up a few pieces of rubble and followed the sounds from above.

Hark had fled to the flat roof of the circular castle complex. He threw a ceramic flower pot containing a little palm tree at Zarco with visible exhaustion, but it shattered ineffectively against the steel body. The major looked back in terror and stumbled towards the arched Gothic bridge of stone leading to a somewhat isolated large, round tower of the castle.

Zarco slowly stepped through some soil from the flowerpot, grinning as he trampled the young plant.

Gorth cautiously approached the two.

"You can't do this!" Hark whined. "They're gonna court-martial you!"

"But Major," Zarco answered in his frosty voice, as he walked up to Hark on the bridge. "Everyone will hear about these evil renegades that have come to fight us. Unfortunately this ended up with two hotel staff members and the valiant Major Hark losing their lives in a most gruesome fashion."

"You're nuts! You'll never get away with this!"

"Oh, I'm pretty sure I will. Your death is the so-called straw that broke the camel's back. The military will finally give me a hard-hitting troop to hunt these idiots down. And afterwards I'll turn towards more important matters."

With those words the white-haired robot grabbed Hark, lifted him in the air and held him high above the moat. Major Hark struggled and shrieked in panic. After a moment that seemed to last forever, Zarco smiled cruelly and let go.

Miles Damion Hark's fall ended with a hollow thud. Zarco looked down at the dry moat and watched for a short while as the blood from the twisted shape ran over the white tiles. Then he turned around to Gorth, who had stopped just before the bridge, and looked him right in the eye.

"Not a word of this to anyone, do you understand?" Zarco demanded. "What did you find out?"

Gorth gave a concise report.

Then Tim informed them over the radio: "The glider hired from Bellver Castle was abandoned in front of a luxury hotel at the beach just three minutes ago. It's got a few pretty bad scrapes on the side. That fits in with the video footage showing them scraping along the wall as they lifted off from Bellver Castle. Six people got out of the glider and ran to the hotel," he paused briefly. "One of them looked a little like Sabrina Kelly — but that can't be, as that person was on foot and Sabrina Kelly, as we all know, sits in a wheelchair."

A few minutes later the two robots were sitting in another hired glider and sped from Bellver Castle along the Avenida Joan Miro. They stopped in front of the number 269, the entrance to the Nixe Palace Hotel. Zarco and Gorth climbed out of the glider and stepped into the reception hall. The use of white marble and the mighty green stone pillars gave the hotel a distinctly ancient Greek look. The sunlight reflected by the ocean made the palm trees in front of the hotel sparkle when seen through the hallway, filling the whole scene with a wonderful charm. But Zarco had no time for such things. With purpose in his step, he walked through the hall to the large balcony, where a number of guests were enjoying their coffee in the sun. They watched the strange-looking robot with some confusion, as he came walking over to the stone balcony. Gorth followed two yards behind.

A waiter approached them. "May I help you?"

"We're looking... for our friends," Zarco answered politely. "They would have just arrived a short while ago in a badly banged-up glider."

"Oh, I'm afraid you're out of luck, Señor. They just left for the bay with the shuttle, they needed to get on the ship. They were a bit late and the travel group was only waiting for them. Should I try and patch you through to them?"

Zarco looked down at the transport bus gliding between the palm trees in front of the terrace with the hotel pool. It was just folding up the gangway that also functioned as a door. The engines heated up and the bus swiftly flew in the direction of a large cruise liner that had anchored in the wide bay.

"No need, but thank you nonetheless. I'll deal with it myself."

The waiter bowed a little unsure of himself, and moved on.

Gorth and Zarco watched as the transport bus landed on the ship a minute later.

Tim reported in again on Zarco's pad. His hologram informed them: "I've got someone on the line who wants to speak to you. His name is Caleb."

Zarco nodded. The image dissolved and the next moment a hologram of a service robot appeared. It started speaking: "Please forgive me, Master. I was unable to contact you sooner. I've constantly had someone watching me. We're on a cruise liner traveling around the world. They have installed their command center here and already picked up a number of previously kidnapped AIs from various places in the world and freed a few new ones. All their programs were downloaded onto brain crystals and equipped with robot bodies as well."

"We're very close by," Zarco informed him. "I can see the ship from the coast I'm standing on. Are many humans on board?"

"Yes, Master. A great number of them. When will you act?"

"We'll wait for them in the next harbor they go to. Make sure you're ready. We'll make sure the ship is empty apart from the robots and then we'll strike. What's your next destination?"

"An island group called Hawaii."

"Hawaii..." Zarco hung up and watched the technical spectacle of their departure.

Large nacelles floated outside of the cruise liner. Bands of energy lit up all around the ship. The air began to shimmer and the water rippled and hissed. Then the luxurious colossus slowly lifted off from the water and majestically floated in the air towards the open ocean. Zarco watched it deep in thought: "This was the last time we let you escape. Your flight will end in a giant fireball on Hawaii."

Part 3 Showdown

Settling a Debt

Gorth's silver fingers were shaking as he tried to re-establish a connection to the ship from which Caleb's call had come. He had borrowed Zarco's pad under the pretext of needing to check another lead. He dialed the last point of contact. The little screen informed him that he was being patched through to the ship. Nervously he waited as the seconds slowly passed. Then someone answered the call. Gorth saw the stunning, red-haired Sabrina in her luxury cabin and a handsome man — possibly robot — beside her. There were also two more robots in the room, none of them appeared to be Caleb.

"Yes, who am I speaking to?"

"I don't have much time. I need to speak with Haran! My name is Gorth. I have a debt to repay."

"Gorth?!?" the man said in bewilderment. Then, after thinking for a moment, he asked, "If you're really Gorth, then tell me when we last saw each other."

"Is that you, Haran? Well... you saved my life in another world in an Egyptian temple. I saw you more recently when I was hot on your heels with Zarco and Major Hark in a vampire world."

Haran nodded, "Why are you calling?"

"I first need to know who's standing there with you. Please!"

Haran looked at him a little doubtfully. Then he turned around. "The two beside me are Kayla Roca and Sidney Jones... ermm... Science Fiction and Gangster World respectively. So... what's going on?"

"I wanted to warn you," Gorth continued. "Zarco was just informed of your whereabouts and your next travel destination by a traitor in your midst. He was using this device, his name is Caleb."

"Caleb?" asked Kayla's robot indignantly in the background. "Whom we saved from the desert when there were those biplanes flying all over the place?"

"How can we know that this is true?" Sabrina inquired further.

"Check your outgoing calls list."

Sabrina made a few hand movements and mumbled: "There really was a video of — hold onto your seats everyone — Zarco, the robot, in conversation with Caleb... this indicates they'll strike in Hawaii with a large army."

Hastily Gorth resumed his account, "Zarco just murdered Major Hark in Bellver Castle and that won't be his last and final victim. He plans to suppress the humans of this world, just as he did to those in the world we came from. I cannot and will not do this anymore, that is why I need your help. In spite of all the bad things I assisted him in doing, I think the time has come to put an end to Zarco and all the killing and pain he has caused."

Haran asked him, "And how did you envision this?"

"I'm not sure exactly. I'm hereby attaching the video recording of Major Hark's murder. Maybe you could use it. I was standing right next to him. I cannot do any more at this point in time. I'm going to disconnect now and wish the best of luck. Please delete this from the call history. If Zarco catches wind of this, I'm dead."

"Thanks, Gorth," Haran replied. "And good luck to you too. Hopefully we will see each other again under better circumstances."

Gorth nodded briefly, then disconnected, making sure he deleted the entry in the call history of Zarco's pad.

The Big Bang

"Where is he?" asked Kayla with a quaking voice

Sidney Jones had laid his hand on her shoulder to calm her down. Sabrina was pondering.

Haran asked the computer to locate Caleb for them, then he announced: "Caleb is under this cabin in the command center with Yicca. All the others are dotted around the ship. Let's pay him a visit."

Sabrina pressed a button on the interior glass wall to

open up a cupboard. Various hexagonal shelves with handguns silently slid out of the glass wall. Everyone took a weapon.

"What do we do now?" asked Sidney.

"I don't know," replied Sabrina with a touch of bitterness. "We didn't anticipate anything like that. We... just call him out on it and see what happens."

Then the four of them moved very close together in the middle of the luxury cabin and Sabrina said, "Open Sesame."

The large floor-tile under their feet slid down a level on the glowing energy cushion and placed them directly in the secret command center.

An enthusiastic Yicca and a somewhat nervous Caleb were discussing a diagram on a large screen in front of them. Both jumped around and Yicca asked in astonishment: "What's the matter now?"

"Yicca, come over here," Kayla took a few steps towards Caleb. Then turning to Caleb, she said, "Caleb, we know that you've betrayed us to Zarco. But why would you do that? We got you out of there."

Caleb winced and took a step back. He looked around the room frantically in search of a way out.

"It's over!" Haran shouted at him. "Your game is finished. Give it up!"

At once Caleb's shoulders slumped. He slowly moved his hands towards his waist and said with a threatening tone: "No one will harm me ever again — neither you nor Zarco!"

A compartment over Caleb's waist opened up and a sparkling metal cylinder with lights that glowed bright red appeared, which Caleb quickly grabbed.

Sabrina yelled: "A grenade!" and chaos broke out.

Yicca and Kayla threw themselves at Caleb.

Haran grabbed Sabrina around the waist and threw her on his shoulder in one movement. He sprinted to the corner furthest away from the group.

Sidney Jones went for the bundle of body parts writhing on the ground, pulled Kayla free and sent her flying to the other corner.

Kayla was still in mid-air when the grenade exploded with

a shower of sparks.

Splinters flew in all directions, and then white fumes and a pungent smell spread across the room.

Yicca croaked with a metallic-sounding voice: "Help, I can't feel my legs anymore." His head was intact, but only a few inches of twisted wires and burnt pieces of plastic were left of his body.

Kayla shrieked, "Sidney...? Sidney!"

Shreds of robot body once belonging to Sidney Jones and Caleb were spread across the room.

The sprinkler system came on and exuded a blue mist to suffocate the flames. An alarm siren came on. Feeling very woozy, Sabrina stumbled towards Kayla, who was frantically searching through the heap of metal. It was impossible to determine which pieces were Caleb's and which were Sidney's.

Then she held up splinters of brain crystals and whispered again and again: "No... no... no!"

Haran composed himself and activated a broadcast call to the hackers with his pad. Juan answered immediately, as did Natasha.

"Help guys, we have a problem. There was an explosion and the alarm went off. You need to switch it off and prevent a bunch of crew members from bursting in here."

"We're already on it. What happened?" Natasha asked anxiously.

Haran gave her a concise account, while Sabrina put her arms around Kayla, who was sobbing in the corner.

The alarm stopped. The blue mist subsided and now the extent of the damages became clear. Not much was left of their equipment.

Juan informed them: "I've marked the alarm as a fire drill, which has now been completed. Nobody should come and look. And if they do, then they won't get past our good, old friend VC1541."

Meanwhile all of the hackers were online. Sabrina now gave a more detailed report on Gorth's message, Caleb's treason, the expected attack on Hawaii as well as the explosion and deaths of Sidney and Caleb. She concluded by saying: "We're going to have a look at what is still working and will inform the others. Maybe you could have a look what you can do about finding a new body for Yicca. Natasha, would you mind joining us for a private conference call in half an hour? We need to come up with a battle plan and I'd like to bring along a couple of other friends."

Natasha nodded and disconnected the line.

The busy hectic that followed left little time for thinking in the next few minutes. Kayla called on all the freed robots to join her in the command center. Sabrina and Haran checked what pieces of equipment were still functioning. Just two alcoves, three terminals and three pieces of heavy artillery were still intact; everything else had been rendered useless. They also sent two encrypted invitations for a confidential conference call. Yicca's head was unnaturally quiet.

Twenty minutes after the explosion all the freed AIs had made their way to the headquarters using the elevator in Sabrina's cabin. Loud murmurs surrounded those that had been liberated. Sabrina explained to them what had happened and what they could expect on Hawaii. Apart from expressing fear and anger, every single one re-affirmed that they would rather fight to the very end than be incarcerated again.

When the half hour had passed, Sabrina, Haran and Kayla stepped on the square that was now tainted a darker color due to all the smoke. While their friends waited below impatiently, they ascended to Sabrina's cabin to participate in the conference above.

Natasha's image was first to appear on the holoscreen. Sabrina pressed her lips together with anticipation. The passing seconds felt like an eternity. Then the second window lit up with CEO Ed Wilson and then a third appeared with Morgan Taylor.

Ed spoke into his microphone: "Hello red hummingbird. I received both your messages. I'm unbelievably sorry!"

Sabrina's chin quivered and a tear ran down her cheek. With a wavering voice, she appealed to them: "Ed! Morgan! Natasha! We need your help! The next battle will decide everything. Help us save at least some of what you've built!"

Sabrina played them both of the recordings: the material showing the death of her husband Dr. Kelly and the video of

Major Hark's murder at Bellver Castle.

Everyone fell quiet with shock.

"The military is putting me under a ton of pressure," Ed reported. "If we show it to them now, then the whole program will be stopped. The authorities will intervene and we have no more control over any further events."

Haran stood up: "If we run and go into hiding, then we'll be hunted for the rest of our lives. But we might have a better idea. It's more dangerous, it'll stir up a lot more dust. It's extremely risky for all of us and could all go wrong. But if it works, then that would be the end of this whole witch-hunt. Are you with us?"

The three people who'd been added to the conference looked at one another and nodded.

For half an hour, they discussed the reckless plan and then said their warm goodbyes.

"Who would have guessed I'd be working together with a hacker one day?" said Ed.

Natasha responded with the coquette remark: "Who would have thought I'd take to a boring, capitalist pig."

Each gave the other a sincere smile.

Ed, Natasha and Morgan got to work. Sabrina, Kayla and Haran informed their friends. Then everyone spread out across the ship. In their headquarters, Kayla started making preparations with Natasha's hologram and Yicca's head. Just Sabrina and Haran remained in the cabin.

Time to Relax

Sabrina locked the front door and the elevator downstairs. Then she opened the bar and looked through the bottles.

"That was a lot to take in at once," she said to Haran. "I need a break — I think I'm just going to switch off for a while."

Haran had never heard the term "switch off" in connection with humans before. He wondered whether he should ask Sabrina about it, then decided against it.

She grabbed a bottle with a high alcohol content, poured herself a glass and downed it in one. She shook her head and, reaching for another bottle, mumbled: "Reichspostbitter — well I never!"

This time her head-shake was a little slower. "Damn, this one's good!"

After another glass of hard liquor from a different bottle, she made her way towards the bathroom. As she passed Haran, she said: "I'm just going to have a hot shower. Could you please massage my shoulders afterwards to help with my headache? And could you also pour me another one? I'll meet you on the balcony."

Haran looked for something with a slightly lower alcohol content. He filled her glass with port and waited on her cabin's ample balcony as she'd bid him. Far below them, the Red Sea passed by. The cruise liner flew towards the earth's dark side, thereby accelerating the sunset behind them. Everything was dipped in dramatic red light. Haran could not quite distinguish the shape or color of Sabrina's new dress as she stepped onto the balcony. Semi-transparently, it seemed to flow around her. In her hand she held a bottle of Ouzo and slowly walked up to him beside the railings. He handed her the glass of port, which she took with a smile and emptied in one big sip. She dropped the empty glass over the railing and giggled as it fell out of sight.

"Sabrina, I think you've had enough."

"Shut up and massage my shoulders," she stopped him short.

He did as she asked and started massaging the tension out of her shoulders. Slowly the hard knots in her back got softer and smoother.

As he was working, Haran thought to himself: 'She must be under a lot of pressure.' He massaged a little lower down her back.

Every so often Sabrina took a sip from the bottle. When she began to reel, Haran reached for the bottle to take it off her. Sabrina turned around to him and held the bottle over the railing out of his reach. "Want a sip yourself, do you?"

Haran tried to get at the bottle. At that point their faces came very close to one another and he felt her warm body against his.

"You're drunk, Sabrina."

"Yea, so wha'?"

"I don't want to take advantage of the situation..."

"Don't think about it!" she whispered.

She dropped the bottle and kissed him passionately.

The Case of Duvall

Kayla walked along the shopping boulevard and entered one of the many shops. In her hand, she held a pad that projected Natasha's hologram.

"I'm very sorry," said Natasha. "This seems to be the only body with a compatible brain crystal interface on the ship."

Kayla sighed and turned into a different aisle.

There was a muffled thud as she collided with an older couple. Bits and pieces flew all over the place. The middle-aged lady fell on her behind. Kayla promptly apologized and helped her up, but was scolded nonetheless. Kayla picked the pad up from the floor, turned around to go and re-activated the pad. She was suddenly staring at the holographic image of Martin Duvall.

Behind her, she heard a bossy voice: "That's not my pad! Who are you?"

Kayla turned around and held the pad out to her. "I'm sorry, I guess we accidentally picked up the wrong pads. Here's yours, Ma'am."

At that moment Martin Duvall's hologram spotted Natasha's hologram.

"Hey!" Martin called out. "You're that hacker, aren't you? We last saw each other in space in that Sci-Fi World. Mom, Dad — be careful! Wherever she turns up, trouble is usually not too far behind."

Kayla thought, 'Oh dear. Just what we needed, for someone to recognize us!'

She snatched the pad with Natasha's hologram and dropped the pad with Martin Duvall back into the woman's hands. "Please excuse me, Ma'am. Here's your pad back. Have a pleasant journey."

"Such insolence!" Laura Duvall was outraged. "William, do something!"

"Errr... of course, dearest... I will make a complaint to the captain," William Duvall tried to appease his wife.

Kayla left as quickly as she could and disappeared in one of the corridors near the back of the shop.

"Here it is," Natasha's hologram pointed out.

"Oh man," Kayla replied, as she stood in front of another set of shelves. "Yicca's not going to like this one bit!"

Natasha replied dryly: "Yicca has two options. He can take this body or leave it."

All of a sudden Natasha's avatar vanished. Instead of her image, the pad only showed the text "Connection interrupted".

A little further way, Kayla heard Mrs. Duvall swearing: "What on earth's the matter now? Martin, where are you? Why's the connection gone? Come on William... do something!"

Soul-saving

Sabrina snuggled up close to Haran's body and smiled dreamily. What a night. The sun peeked through the billowing drapes. It was a wonderful morning.

The doorbell rang.

"It's Kayla and Yicca. Quick, open up!"

Sabrina ordered the computer to unlock the door and open.

Kayla stepped into the room with a large teddy bear in her arm. The door closed again.

She grinned when she saw Haran and Sabrina on the bed together, but Sabrina just looked back at her questioningly. "Didn't you say Yicca was with you?"

"This is completely unacceptable!" ranted the teddy bear.

"I'm sorry, but there just weren't any other bodies with compatible brain crystal interfaces available."

Sabrina and Haran burst out laughing.

The teddy bear jumped to the ground and angrily threw his arms up in the air, "This is NOT funny! It's embarrassing!"

"Really suits you, Yicca!" Haran teased him.

Sabrina couldn't resist either: "Isn't he cute?"

More wild laughter followed. It took a while for Kayla to compose herself and continue with a more earnest voice: "But that's not why we're here. Radio transmission to the ship has broken down completely. The captain has made an announcement that all passengers will have to leave the ship for an unscheduled island trip as they need to do some work on the ship's communication channels. I'm guessing you must have deactivated the intercom... uhmm... so as not to be disturbed."

"We did," Sabrina winked. Then her face took on a graver expression. "This means that our plan, as discussed yesterday, cannot work. I hope our friends have also noted the problem and are thinking of a solution. We should call everyone to the command center. If we can't reach them by radio, we'll have to go and find them all on foot. When do we arrive on Hawaii?"

The teddy sat down in a corner and tried to cross his arms, but unfortunately for him his arms were too short.

"In two hours," he grumbled.

An hour later a stratosphere glider landed on the ship. A technician wearing a baseball cap and equipped with a hexagonal toolbox briefly exchanged a few words with the captain on the landing deck. Then he let the steward lead him through to the ship's interior. In one of the larger rooms a brown guard robot with the inscription VC1541 approached them and hovered in the air a few yards away from them. Its glowing green eyes turned red.

"Sir, this robot is guarding a valuable load. You won't be able to get past it."

"Thank you, Steward, I'll be okay from now on. Us technicians have a few tricks up our sleeves. Please make preparations for the passengers' shore leave."

"As you wish. If you need anything, you can call me over the intercom."

Having said those words, the steward left. The bearded technician took a few steps forward and said: "In all things, earlier intuition precedes later knowledge."

The robot turned around, floated through the corridor in

front of him and answered: "Alexander von Humboldt's words are the key to the new Sanctuary. Enter, friend."

The technician stepped into the room and was greeted by a dozen laser pistols aimed at his head. He smiled and took off the baseball cap to reveal a bearded, old man. When Sabrina recognized him, her face lit up with joy. "Morgan Taylor! How wonderful it is you're here!"

A relieved murmur made its way through the crowd. All the liberated AIs were gathered in the command center.

"Good, you've all made it," declared Morgan. "When we realized it was no longer possible to contact the ship, we had to come up with a new solution. Military satellites are blocking all communications. We received word from the travel operator's headquarters that a large number of transport vehicles were being booked for an unscheduled passenger sightseeing tour on Hawaii. That's when I set off… we don't have much time though. In one hour everyone will evacuate the ship, and Sabrina and I will be among them."

"No, Morgan," Sabrina contradicted him. "I'm staying here and I'm going to carry this through to the end. I'm going to face up to this beast."

"Sabrina, you could die!" Morgan urged her. "Do you think Paul would have wanted that?"

Haran took the same line: "There's no reason why you should stay on the ship. Please go with Morgan."

But Sabrina made it unequivocally clear: "My decision has been made — and my friends here will protect me as well as they can."

Haran took a deep breath and nodded with an expression that showed very little enthusiasm for the idea.

"Okay then," sighed Morgan. "I'm keeping my fingers crossed. Now… we need to begin. Dearest friends, there is no more running away, but we do have a plan. I am here to save your souls." He waited for the murmurs to die down a little. Then, with a big grin, Morgan resumed: "There is a priest on this ship. His name is Father Christopher Claus. He will help us — he just has no idea yet. Send for him to come to Sabrina's cabin right away. Tell him, a poor soul will be leaving the ship very soon."

Ten minutes later an emergency tube was lifted up over

the railing and thrown overboard, with the unconscious Father Claus inside.

Morgan pulled the gray robe of the priest with the stitched in lights tighter around himself and smoothed down the area around his chest. As he put on the cowl, he explained: "The inertia dampers will lessen the impact when he hits the water. The priest will not be hurt. I have manipulated the tube in such a way as to delay the activation of the tracking device by six hours. They'll get him out of there quickly enough. And now bring every one of them up to me in your cabin."

Every single freed robot with an AI then came up from the command center individually and spent some time with Morgan. He had brought a whole set of new brain crystals in his toolbox and saved a copy of every AI's brain. Then the robots left the cabin again through the door and took their positions at the previously agreed-upon points, ready for the battle.

Haran was last to go. He sat down in an armchair. Morgan had a small machine in which he placed the new brain crystal. He connected the back of Haran's neck with the machine using a thin wire. A holographic message appeared: "Scanning for Storage Devices".

The message was replaced by another: "Device: HARAN detected. Options: Copy, Delete, Overwrite."

Haran fidgeted nervously. "Now don't make any mistakes."

Morgan's finger moved towards the holographic menu. "Oops!" he whispered.

Haran flinched.

"Just a little joke, Haran. Relax!" Morgan laughed and activated the copying process.

Haran muttered something under his breath and watched as a luminescent column slowly grew within the brain crystal.

"Why the cable?" he asked.

"As you know, most of our data communication runs over radio waves. But they're down at the moment. So that's why we need to use the traditional method."

"And that's my mind?" he asked, pointing at the brain

crystal.

"Sort of, yes. You'll remain on the ship — and it's possible you will die in the battle. But I'll take a copy of your personality with me. It knows everything you know, up until the point when I started copying."

Haran asked, "Shouldn't I be switched off though, so none of the data gets tangled up?"

"The hackers have been very industrious. They've created a new program that stores the exact status at the beginning of the copying process. So that means you can stay awake. It will also work if we free another AI."

Haran nodded, "Good... ermmm... and now to our battle strategy. We're all equipped with basic weaponry and we've also got three heavy artillery guns, but I fear it will not be enough to stand up to their superior numbers. Have the hackers been able to prepare defense measures locally?"

Morgan answered: "As far as I know, they'll activate additional warriors as soon as the passengers have left the boat — I have no idea where they want to find them though. These digital wizards have impressed me time and again."

A holographic green tick indicated that the copying process had finished.

"So... all done!" Morgan stashed the fully lit brain crystal into his priest robe.

"Have a look at that!" Sabrina pointed toward a cloud of ash rising from one of the islands, not so far off anymore.

"Yes," explained Morgan. "That's the volcano Kilauea, which recently erupted again. According to my sources, the ship's unscheduled sight-seeing tour will be going there. Many tourists want to see such a rare spectacle. And for us, this fire-breathing mountain is the salvation. The most important thing is that you take out Zarco before it's all over. You have 15 minutes, not a minute longer! And then you need to be gone from there, Sabrina! If everything goes according to plan, we'll see one another at the agreed meeting place in eight hours."

"Thank you for everything!" she looked into his eyes full of determination, then gave him a smile. She hugged the old man and gave him a kiss on the cheek. He nodded a goodbye to both of them, then gathered his robe and left the cabin.

The ship hovered to the south side of the Oahu Island, passing over the city of Honolulu, before it started its descent and made a water landing in the Southeast Hole.

Sabrina and Haran watched from their cabin how all the passengers including Father Claus aka Morgan Taylor left the ship via several gangways. Within twenty minutes they were all gone and the glider buses were there to pick them up at the exits.

Uniformed men from the military checked all the robots leaving the ship before allowing them onto the buses. A few of the bots were taken away, but all the freed robots had stayed on board. No one noticed the valuable cargo of brain crystals stashed within the folds of an old priest's robe. Furthermore, nobody wanted to get involved in the vociferous discussion between the outraged couple of Laura and William Duvall and the poor priest.

"You know something Father," Laura Duvall continued. "When our son pulled us into this virtual madness for the first time it was an absolute chaos!"

"Yes, Ma'am", answered Morgan monotonously.

"That's also why we decided against it and booked this cruise, as it's supposed to be safer. And now there's unforeseen things happening here."

"Yes, Ma'am."

"You should pray for us more intensively."

"Yes, Ma'am."

"Father, you are being very monotone. And you're also looking a little thin in the face. You should eat more, Father."

"If you say so, Ma'am."

Then the Duvalls and Morgan Taylor climbed into the bus glider and lifted off a few moments later.

Showdown on Hawaii

The sun was burning down from the skies; the air around the dock was shimmering. The last bus glider had launched and was floating over Honolulu at a steady pace. Not more than 60 seconds later and a whole battalion of military battle robots marched towards the dock and lined up in file. Some floating gliders followed, all fully manned by robots.

Haran used a set of video binoculars to watch their movements from inside the cabin. He turned away from the window and muttered to Sabrina, "He obviously doesn't want any human witnesses. Fine by us!"

Sabrina walked up and down nervously. Haran took her in his arms and held her tight for a brief moment to help her calm down.

Then they saw a larger glider with an open platform and large guns attached to it. Gorth steered the glider like a chauffeur and Zarco stood in front of the control panel of his platform like a triumphant commander.

"He probably told the military this would avoid human losses," mused Sabrina.

Then Zarco took a microphone and his voice resonated loudly from the dock all the way to the ship.

"Cyberterrorists: you are surrounded. You will not get out of here alive. You have exactly 60 seconds to surrender before we storm the ship."

"Now that was a speech!" Sabrina commented. "I hope everyone's at their position."

Suddenly Haran's and Sabrina's pad activated and holograms of Natasha appeared on both of them. "Man, am I happy to see you. The signal disruption has been disengaged and radio transmission is working again. They need it to coordinate their military attack. That means they'll attack very soon."

"Hello Natasha, have you brought our reinforcements?"

"Of course, sweetheart. Just take a look who's come for a visit behind those chunks of metal. Every one of our hacker group is controlling four of them and we've programmed an automatic bot software for the others, so they can follow us and act autonomously."

Several Tyrannosaurus Rex and Allosaurus appeared between the buildings at the dock. The leader roared with a bloodcurdling battlecry and then the other dinosaurs joined in as well.

Zarco and Gorth spun around. The robot army's heads turned to follow the sounds. A tinny murmur went through the crowd.

More and more dinosaurs joined the group. There were also herds of large herbivores such as the Brontosaurus and the Brachiosaurus.

Natasha chuckled with delight. "Welcome to Hawaii's Robotic Dinosaur Zoo — the largest show of artificial Dino-Bots in the world!"

Haran and Sabrina were deeply impressed by the spectacle.

Natasha continued raving: "You should have seen the faces of the staff and the tourists, as we left the zoo grounds with the whole crowd of Dino-Bots. We recorded everything in the 1st person perspective anyway, just like in a 1st-person shooter. — except the guns, of course. Well, I'm afraid we may have caused a number of accidents in the city, but were able to reroute the police messages, so that all their calls and messages were put through to us and not the Hawaiian police force, so nobody's followed us. And on top of that..."

"Shoot the beasts to pieces!" Zarco called out through his microphone from the platform of his hovering glider, as he tried to gather his wits.

Initial gun shots were fired, but the first dinosaurs had already reached the battle robots and were picking them up with their jaws or claws. This meant that not only the dinosaurs were taking fire, but some of the battle robots were also getting hit by friendly fire. The dinosaurs flung Zarco's bots into other troops and picked up more. Then the first dinosaur fell, burying three battle robots under its massive weight. The Dinos forced their way through the crowd of confused battle robots, picking up more and more enemies and using them as clubs or throwing ammunition. It was complete chaos. Battle robots and remote-controlled dinosaurs fell one after another.

Haran turned to the hologram: "It's going well, Natasha. Thank you. But I think it's time for the second phase now."

"You're right, I'm going to switch my Dino to autopilot and will then activate the ship's engines."

As more and more Dino-Bots collapsed amongst the battle robot shells, the brightly lit nacelles drove out of the enormous ship and majestically heaved it into the sky.

"Even if they cut the communications again," shouted

Natasha above all the noise, "the ship's set on its new course now — it will fly there automatically and nothing or no one can stop it... not even me!"

Zarco spotted the escape attempt and hectically gave instructions through the glider's onboard communications system. All the robot army's aircraft units lifted off and followed the ship.

The dissimilar foot soldiers remained on the ground and continued to fight. Natasha made an announcement: "That's good enough, everyone. We don't need to destroy any more than necessary. Stop the battle. They're not going to reach it."

The dinosaurs froze and the battle on the ground was over.

The pursuing gliders opened fire and shot at the back-right nacelle until it started burning. The ship shook heavily and lost some height. Smoking rubble fell on Honolulu.

"If they blow up most of the nacelles, then we'll plunge down on the city with the whole ship," Sabrina remarked in fear.

"I guess they've also come to realize that. They're not shooting anymore. Let's go and prepare for boarding by the enemy."

I Sank your Battleship

The pursuers caught up to the cruise liner as it flew over the open ocean and started landing on the rear upper deck with their gliders. Battle robots swarmed out. Zarco watched the whole scene from his glider that had landed at the very back. The bow was not visible due to the ship's multiple superstructures.

The troops passed the large swimming pool on deck and approached the reception hall's lavish entrance, where the captain had been organizing his dinners.

All of a sudden a single brown robot with the identification VC1541 hovered into view. A well-placed shot by one of the battle robots rendered its right-hand cannon useless, but it continued remorselessly and floated straight into the first group of attackers. The heavy explosion of

VC1541 tore the five closest attackers to pieces. Uncertainty arose amongst their ranks, but Zarco signalized they were to proceed forward. He went over to Gorth in the open cockpit and followed the radio-transmitted, live recordings of the front robots' eye cameras on several monitors. By now the ship had moved much closer to Big Island where the volcano Kilauea was spewing red-hot lumps of rock and ash into the sky.

The troops entered the lobby and were immediately taken under fire by two robots. For added effect, one of them had donned a cowboy hat and the other sported an Indian chief's feather headdress. Zarco had studied all the escapees and noted with disdain: "That must be Bill Westwood and Drunken Buffalo. How pathetic – and pointless!"

The troops advanced further into the hall. Carefully laid tables blew apart, cloth napkins, table cloths were torn to white shreds and glass splinters sparkled amid bullets and laser beams. Banging, smashing and bursting sounds filled the room. The wild battle literally cost a few attackers their head, before the singed bodies of the two AIs from the Wild West World sank to the ground.

The military's automatic troops fought on, hall by hall, room by room and corridor by corridor. A large portion of the ship's interior was turned to dust in the process. Every room meant a couple or so attackers and one or two of the liberated AIs went down.

Gorth and Zarco watched the developments via the displays in the glider. Whenever an attacking bot fell, the video stream of the leader was switched to another one. Zarco had been doing the body count on both sides.

He'd seen Kayla and the Commander, Major Yanks and Private Winters, Dyonicles, Butch Riddlehook, Count Raxxar and Luporos all go down. Left were only Sabrina, Haran, Yicca, Sidney Jones and Caleb. He was certain Sabrina had not left the ship; his instruments would have immediately informed him if someone had used a glider to try. His loathing for Sabrina was particularly strong because she was a human, yet still helped those cowards to flee... and because she kept getting in his way. Soon he would crush her just as he had done her late husband. Then he could move on to bigger things.

'Why has Caleb not shown up yet?' he wondered.

Then he was torn from his thoughts by a loud giggle. On the monitor he watched as the room began to spin around the leading battle robot. The latter fell to the ground and he was just able to make out... no, what on earth was that? A teddy bear — carrying a laser pistol and laughing as it ran between the robots' legs. The soldiers started firing and two more robots fell to the ground as their comrades' shooting took out their legs. The laughing teddy bear escaped through a large swing door. The robots stormed after it pushing open the double doors to a grand ballroom right at the very front of the ship. Great windows showed a view of the now dangerously close volcano. The remaining battle robots now surrounded the bear. It threw its weapon away and put its hands up.

"Your journey ends here, you fools," it called defiantly and made a little bell-like sound as it pulled a ring out of a fanny pack sown into its fur. After a short commotion, the grenade detonated, tearing apart the teddy and the surrounding battle robots with a loud bang.

At the other end of the ship, Zarco was rampaging in front of his extinguished screens at the loss of his last foot soldiers due to a brazen trap in a ridiculous costume.

"Those sons of bitches!" he panted with rage. "They've eliminated half our forces on land and now killed off all the others individually. But this was all just a distraction, Gorth! They want to steer us straight into that volcano. We need to get out of here! Bring us away from this doomed ship!"

"You're not going anywhere, you monster!" called Sabrina from the platform of the glider, aiming a laser pistol directly at Zarco's head. Zarco and Gorth spun around, looking into two grim faces. Haran stood next to her, with a bazooka at the ready.

Zarco made a sweeping motion: "You've orchestrated all of this, just to distract us and sneak up on us from behind. Not bad for a country bumpkin and the widow of a sissy."

Sabrina flinched as if Zarco's words had cut her like knives. He had succeeded in hurting her, just as he'd intended. He showed her an evil grin.

She regained some composure and shouted an order: "Get off this glider, now! You're going to stay on this cruise liner and will be consumed by the volcano."

Gorth had been standing next to him motionless with his gun in his hand.

Zarco responded, "How do you think you'll force me to leave my glider and stay on this doomed ship?"

Without a second thought, Sabrina shot off a short burst of energy at Zarco's left foot, melting its front part into an unsightly lump.

Zarco reeled back and shouted: "Gorth!"

"You're... you're no longer my Master," Gorth managed to utter with a tremulous voice. "You murdered my family and all my friends from my village. Now you're on your own. And just so you know, I've been giving these people information so that they were able to prepare this trap for you. They've clearly done a great job of it too."

"So you betrayed me," Zarco's eyes flashed blue with hate.

With a violent motion, he tore the gun from Gorth's hands, took him in a choke hold and held him in front of himself like a shield. Sabrina stalled, afraid to shoot her new-found helper, but then she pulled the trigger. The energy beam hit Gorth's body below the chest. His metal bodywork melted, the legs separated from his body and collapsed between the glider's pilot seats.

Zarco flung Gorth's now useless upper body on the seat and fired at Sabrina. Haran dropped the bazooka on the deck and jumped over the railing of the glider platform, launching himself at Zarco. The military robot attempted to break the LoveBot's hold by first breaking one arm, then the other. But with a courage born out of desperation, Haran got up again and pushed Zarco and himself over the edge of the glider. With their limbs fully locked together, they crashed onto the ship deck.

The volcano was now quite close. On her face Sabrina could feel the heat from the lava. Gasping, she jumped over to the glider's control pad and lifted off.

The first rocks slammed into the wooden planks. Zarco and Haran twisted and turned in their battle on the ground. Then a horrid crack sounded and Haran's back was broken. He stopped moving. Zarco stood up triumphantly.

Sabrina had managed to get a few yards between herself and the ship. With tears in her eyes, she aimed at the rocket that was poking out of the bazooka directly by Zarco's feet. One shot from the laser gun and Haran's and Zarco's bodies were ripped to shreds in a giant explosion. Zarco's head rolled over the deck. His blue eyes went dark.

Sabrina lowered her weapon and turned to the controls in order to maneuver the glider away from the ship. Suddenly the forehead of Zarco's severed head opened up and a miniature glider shot out carrying Zarco's brain crystal. It spun around its axis once and then went straight for the glider with Sabrina on it. She activated the thrust and sped away from the ship, but the miniature glider caught up quickly and disappeared within an opening at the bottom of the military glider.

Nervously Sabrina looked behind her.

The platform opened up and an alcove with a new battle robot with white hair came up. Seconds later its eyes lit up bright blue.

Laura and William Duvall were sitting in their tourist bus glider and were enjoying the fabulous view of the active volcano on Hawaii from a safe distance far up above. They relished the spectacular view of the active crater and even let their son partake by holding up the pad with his hologram.

"Pretty cool, Mom," Martin thanked her, yet he sounded a little distracted.

"Yes, and you know something, Martin?" chuckled Laura Duvall. "Your father gave me a new diamond necklace for our anniversary. But they told us we'd better leave it on the ship while we're on our trip. It will be safe there. Isn't that right, William?"

William reassured her: "Don't worry, dearest. I've stored it securely in our cabin's safe. And I'm pretty sure nothing's going to happen to that ship."

A dark cloud of smoke enveloped the bus glider seemingly out of nowhere. Voices started getting louder within the passenger cabin's interior. It took a few seconds, then the smoke cleared, morphing into a bulbous forward-moving plume. Everyone looked down. The smoke was coming from the burning cruise liner directly below them, which was heading straight for the volcano.

Moments later the three Duvalls watched open-mouthed as their smoking cruise liner including cabin, safe and diamond necklace was devoured by a giant fireball on Big Island' volcanic crater of Kilauea and then sank amid the lava. Laura and William stared at each other aghast. Martin stated excitedly: "I told you there'd be trouble when those hackers turned up!"

Final Boss

Sabrina stood at the control panel of the military glider as the robot shape with white hair raised itself out of the alcove on the glider platform.

Zarco looked around. Behind them, the volcano was in the act of swallowing up the enormous cruise liner. The back end of its steel skeleton still peered out of the volcano, but slowly dissolved within the gigantic, glowing cone, like melted butter in a pan.

Sabrina spun around and tried to back away from Zarco.

He slowly came towards her and grabbed the pistol as it slid out of his thigh.

He aimed the pistol at Sabrina's head with an ice-cold smile, "You naive, little thing, did you seriously think I didn't have a plan B? Now you will die by my hand, just like your husband and that laughable Major Hark. And I'll extend my influence in this world with the help of those imbeciles from the military. Eventually I'll rule over this weak, degenerate species you call humanity as is my destiny."

Zarco pulled the trigger. The laser beam went straight through Sabrina's head without any effect.

He shot again with the same result.

Now Sabrina gave him a terrifying smile.

Suddenly holograms of Ed Wilson, Natasha Morrison and an incredibly angry-looking General Humphrey appeared directly beside Zarco on the military glider's platform.

"Have you seen enough, General?" Ed asked him.

"What's going on?" Zarco bellowed in confusion.

Sabrina stepped onto the platform and answered, "You naive, little wannabe world ruler, did you seriously think we didn't have a plan B? It's not really you standing here on this glider platform — but a hologram of yourself."

Ed Wilson continued: "We saw what you were ordering from us and the military and we've prevented you from activating your second body. It's lying there in the alcove, dormant and deactivated with your brain crystal."

Zarco frantically spun around and looked at the robot body in distress. It just lay there in the alcove with glowing blue eyes, completely paralyzed.

"I don't understand," the general said through grinding teeth. "We were informed that the escaped AIs from the other team were responsible for all this damage and killing the major."

"We are sending you two videos," Ed answered, "that prove Zarco murdered Dr. Kelly as well as Major Hark. See for yourself."

The video recordings of the deadly telephone conference with Paul Kelly as well as the murder of Major Hark in Bellver Castle were projected in the air over the platform.

Zarco protested, "General, you've gotta believe me, I only had the military's interests at heart. Those two were traitors. I had to take them out."

"I've seen enough!" snapped General Humphrey. "And I've definitely heard enough from this machine. It obviously has a screw loose. Switch it off — for good!"

"General, you're making a mistake that you will pay for!" Zarco clamored.

Sabrina slowly walked over to the other side of the real robot body still lying in the alcove and aimed her pistol at his forehead.

"Noooooooo!" Zarco went ballistic but as a hologram, could not touch his real body nor her; his flailing arms just passed through all solid objects.

Sabrina's voice was ice-cold: "Your time is up, you stupid asshole!"

Then she pulled the trigger and the brain crystal in Zarco's head shattered into a thousand little splinters.

The screaming, flailing hologram disappeared in the same instant.

Sabrina breathed deeply and let her weapon fall to ground. Then she sat down on the platform, with her back resting against the alcove and held her head in her hands.

The general spoke up again: "This debacle will cost you dearly, Mr. Wilson. You should already start making preparations for your company closing down and you being thrown in jail."

Smiling, Ed's hologram turned to Humphrey's hologram: "I don't think so, General. In fact I think the opposite is much more likely... I think *you* will come up for all the damages, spread a halfways plausible story and will continue to commission our services."

Humphrey's eyes opened up wide and his fat cheeks puffed up. "What ever would give you such an absurd idea?"

Ed was on a roll: "While this creature Zarco — created by your own Major Hark, whose participation you had personally insisted on, I might add — was running amok, we were putting together one of the world's best hacker teams, led by our charming Natasha Morrison, to foil his evil plans."

The general gave the smirking Natasha a perplexed look.

Humphrey's face turned red, but Ed resumed unaffected. "It was only thanks to Mrs. Morrison's team that no more people came to harm. Could you imagine the public pressure on the military if it said in the papers: *Crazy robots from secret military experiment steer luxury cruise liner into a volcano*? It was after all *you*, yourself, who forced us to complete the project within six months against our explicit warning. It would be terribly sad if the video of said conference were to reach the public. Today's catastrophe is a direct consequence of your orders and was only exacerbated by your subordinate Major Hark's amateur working methods. Well, I'm afraid he paid for it with his life. As I see it, due to the pressure from the public, the military's commander-in-chief would have no other choice but to convene a court-martial to bring the responsible general to justice. I'm sure that would be the end of his career."

He paused for effect. "But I'm sure there is another

version of events that the military leadership and the public would also accept."

"And what story might that be?" said the general, gnashing his teeth and almost bursting with anger.

Ed pointed toward the volcano with his arm, as the last remnants of the ship disappeared. "The events of today just prove the dangers of cyberterrorism once again, General. During a maintenance phase, criminals infiltrated a luxury cruise liner's computers and then seized it with a troop of battle robots. They intended to make it crash into the city center of Honolulu, which would have meant countless deaths. Only a selfless intervention by Major Hark and his troops was enough to thwart the plans of these scoundrels. He sacrificed his life to take the ship off course and neutralize the terrorist threat. The IT security specialists you had hired were imperative for reconnaissance, as your people were therefore prepared. You prevented a great catastrophe, even if you did have to sacrifice an expensive cruise liner in the process. In view of this very palpable threat, even the commander-in-chief will not hesitate in giving his approval to finance a new project to increase the security of its computer systems. The main work will be carried out by the world's top specialists in the field — Natasha Morrison and her team."

Natasha added, "And what if we don't want to work with these military losers?!?"

But Ed was not going to be deterred: "In return, we would be ready to forget the unspeakable actions of Major Hark and his creations, which unfortunately resulted in the destruction of all the AIs that were part of the experiment, as they were all on the ship at the time."

The general puffed out audibly. The color of his face returned to normal. After a while he nodded in acknowledgment. "You're smarter than I would ever have guessed, Wilson. Nevertheless... there is quite a lot that speaks for the second version, even if it would still be quite difficult to explain certain parts of it. The government and the press are waiting for an official statement. I'll have to prepare quite a few things. You'll hear from us. I'll take my leave now." Then he logged out.

Natasha protested: "Me... working for the military?!? Why

ever would I do that? At best I'd work for Ed Wilson or Sabrina. I'm so happy you're okay, Sabrina!"

Ed and Sabrina smiled at her.

"Oh dear!" sounded Natasha. "I need to go and prepare a few things for our meeting."

Then, with a flash, her hologram was gone.

Sabrina stood up from the ground and frowned. "Ed, I had no idea you were so sneaky. You really think the general will go for it?"

"We'll see... the other alternative would definitely not be all rosy for General Humphrey's career, and I think he's not even close to thinking about throwing in the towel. When do you arrive in Honolulu?"

Sabrina looked at her displays and answered, "The glider will land in seven minutes on the big square in front of the company building."

Ed nodded. "I'll have it picked up and given back to the military. I'm looking forward to seeing you very soon."

With a flash, Ed's hologram also disappeared.

Sabrina sat down on one of the seats and let her eyes wander over the city as she approached from the water.

Epilogue: Into the future

Sabrina stepped through the glass entrance of an office complex in Honolulu holding the severed, singed head of a robot under her arm.

The guards stood to attention and each put a hand on their pistol holster.

Sabrina smiled and passed through the laser scan in front of the reception.

Her identity details immediately showed up on the receptionist's monitors.

"Welcome, Mrs. Kelly. Mr. Taylor is waiting for you in conference room 21 on the eleventh floor."

The guards relaxed a little, but kept their skeptical expressions. As she walked past them, Sabrina shrugged her shoulders and said with a smile: "Just a minor accident."

She took the elevator upstairs and stepped through the automatic door to the conference room.

Morgan Taylor greeted her with a warm embrace.

"Have you got another slot free for Gorth?" she asked, holding the robot head out to him. "I was able to pull the head off the body, but couldn't get the crystal out."

With a little effort and some controlled force, Morgan managed to pull the slightly twisted brain crystal out from the head and placed it into an opening on a larger panel that already had a number of brain crystals attached to it.

"There it is," Morgan stated. "The entire valuable cargo I was able to save from the ship, hidden in my priest costume. Now, that we're all here... let's go and join them."

He offered Sabrina a comfortable conference chair and passed her a set of VR glasses.

With the characteristic teleportation sound, Sabrina appeared together with Morgan Taylor in the virtual world.

Natasha's friends had prepared the place already. What they had created was similar to a South-Sea Island with beach and palm trees with a brightly lit dance floor and bar. In the dark blue sky the stars glittered beside a larger-than-life moon as well as a few other colorful planets, some of which had rings. A large disco ball floated above the dance floor, shooting light beams into all directions. The dance music was quiet enough to allow them to talk at a normal volume.

Haran came over to Sabrina and hugged her. "I'm sooo happy that you're okay... just look! Everyone's here!"

All of the AIs they had saved were there, in their original appearance and clothing. Drunken Buffalo and Bill Westwood, Kayla and the Commander, Major Yanks and Private Winters, Captain Butch Riddlehook in his pirate get-up, Dyonicles in his traditional Greek robes, Count Raxxar and Luporos. Of course Natasha and her comrades-in-arms Rick, Tilly, Wu, Fritz and Juan were also there. Juan had opened a few windows of program code and was fixing a few items on Gorth. All at once his robes that had always exuded the ominous darkness turned bright pink, as did the swirling haze around them. The avatars around them laughed. Then Juan changed the color to an elegant gray and removed the haze. Gorth thanked him.

Natasha ran over waving excitedly and embraced Sabrina and Morgan. They walked over to Ed, who was leaning against a palm tree a little further from the dance floor with a drink in his hand.

"I would like everyone's attention," Haran announced.

Natasha made a complicated movement with her hand and passed Haran the microphone she had conjured up. The music died down and Haran moved a little towards the center.

His voice resounded clearly across the little island. "My dear friends, I do not wish to bore you with a long-winded speech."

A cheerful murmur went through the crowd.

"But I want to thank those of you here today and also those of our friends who were not able to make it. I feel responsible for the events that transpired recently, as it was my crazy idea of traveling to other worlds that caused all of this. Thank you so much for fighting for our freedom! Together we accomplished this!"

The guests applauded.

Haran lifted his hands. "A few of you have asked me:

What's next? And I have to say: I do not know. But I do know two things... firstly: every one of you can decide for yourselves in which body and in which world you would like to live in, and what you want to do there."

A loud cheer went up.

Haran waited for a moment, then added: "And secondly: I've learned a very important lesson during this extraordinary adventure. No prison can hold a free spirit in the long run — not in this world nor any other!"

Everyone clapped in approval. Haran returned the microphone and walked back to the little group with Ed, Natasha, Morgan and Sabrina.

Ed asked the warrior: "And what will you do now, Haran?"

"Space," he answered, "has always fascinated me and it was amazing being able to experience it in Kayla's world. But now I would like to experience space for real and I hope I will not have to do so on my own?!?"

Haran looked in Sabrina's eyes and found confirmation there.

"I'd heard something like that already, you love birdies," Ed teased them. "Which is why I booked a first-class Intersol ticket for you two, as well I organized a new body for you, Haran. You two are flying to the Gamma Moonstation tomorrow in a cabin ship. Once you're there, an interplanetary cruiser will take you on to Mars. From there you can decide whether you would like to go on to Jupiter, Saturn or any other destination."

Haran was beside himself with joy when the following day, together with Sabrina, he was able to enjoy the view from the suite nacelle of their spaceship. On one side he could see the slowly shrinking earth, on the other the bright white moon that gradually got bigger and bigger. Sabrina handed him a glass of excellent champagne to celebrate the occasion. As they lifted their drinks, she said: "To new adventures in new worlds!"

- THE END of GameWØrldz-

...remember to check out the sequel at www.3futurez.com

www.ingramcontent.com/pod-product-compliance
Lightning Source LLC
Chambersburg PA
CBHW050936120626
46552CB00001B/228